Ariel was in danger!

It must have been about three o'clock in the morning when I sat bolt upright in bed. The dogs were barking like crazy. I threw off the covers and ran to the window.

"What's up?" Lydia mumbled groggily. "Tess? Where are you? What's all that noise?"

"It's Nemo and Flash," I told her, struggling to pull up the window sash. "Something's wrong!"

Lydia scurried to my side, and we both stuck our heads out, trying to see what the dogs were so excited about. At first, we didn't see anything unusual. Then suddenly there were horses everywhere, galloping in all directions! The moonlight gleamed on a golden coat and a flowing silvery mane and tail. *Ariel!*

"Somebody must have let them out!" I cried. "We've got to bring them back!"

Collect all the books in the **Thoroughbred** series, by bestselling author Joanna Campbell

#1 *A Horse Called Wonder*
#2 *Wonder's Promise*
#3 *Wonder's First Race*
#4 *Wonder's Victory*

Also by Joanna Campbell

Battlecry Forever!
Star of Shadowbrook Farm

Look for

Christmas Colt by Mallory Stevens,
coming soon.

Available from
HarperPaperbacks

THE PALOMINO

Virginia Vail

HarperPaperbacks

A Division of HarperCollins*Publishers*

For Zachary Landon Brown

This is a work of fiction. The characters, incidents, and
dialogues are products of the author's imagination and are
not to be construed as real. Any resemblance to actual
events or persons, living or dead, is entirely coincidental.

HarperPaperbacks *A Division of* HarperCollins*Publishers*
          10 East 53rd Street, New York, N.Y. 10022

Copyright © 1992 by Daniel Weiss Associates, Inc.
  and Jane Thornton
Cover art copyright © 1992 by Daniel Weiss Associates, Inc.

Produced by Daniel Weiss Associates, Inc.
33 West 17th Street, New York, New York 10011.

First Printing: October, 1992

Printed in the United States of America

HarperPaperbacks and colophon are trademarks of
HarperCollins*Publishers*

10 9 8 7 6 5 4 3 2 1

~1~

Even though it was Labor Day, I didn't actually believe the summer was over until I looked out across the fields and saw splashes of red and gold among the green trees covering the Berkshire foothills.

I was ambling along on Lucky, a bay gelding from my uncle Matthew's rental stable, The Barn. I had spent the whole day helping my uncle lead a group of noisy riders on trails through the Connecticut countryside, just as I'd been doing all summer long. Now Lucky and I were all by ourselves for a change, and I was enjoying the peace and quiet.

Maybe Lucky was too—it was hard to tell with him. Lucky wasn't a very emotional horse, if you know what I mean. He just liked to plod down the road, trying to snatch mouthfuls of greenery when he thought I wasn't paying attention. The only time he pricked up his ears and looked interested was when we started back to the stable. It was as if he could smell the feed waiting for him, even though his stall was more than a mile away.

Don't get me wrong. Maybe Lucky wasn't the most exciting horse in the world, but I loved him and I appreciated his good qualities. He was steady and reliable, which was why I usually chose him for trail rides, and why Matthew let me take him out alone. My uncle is really strict about safety precautions. He hardly ever allows anybody to ride one of his horses without a companion. But he knew that I was a careful, responsible rider—after all, he had taught me himself. Matthew had lifted me onto a pony's back when I was just three years old, and I've been madly in love with horses ever since.

On that September Monday, the late-afternoon sun filtering through the leafy branches overhead still felt summer hot. I wished I could take off my velvet-covered hard hat, but I didn't. That was another of Matthew's safety rules: Nobody rode at The Barn without a protective helmet, in case they fell off and landed on their heads or something. So I just wiped off the sweat that trickled down my forehead, easing the chin strap a little so it didn't cut off my circulation.

That's when I looked up and noticed the red-and-gold trees.

September, I said to myself. *It really is September, and tomorrow is the first day of school. Tomorrow I'll be at*

Stockton High, sitting at a desk instead of riding Lucky or Cinnamon or Frenchie or Baron.

It wasn't a happy thought. This had been the most wonderful summer of my whole fourteen-going-on-fifteen years, and I hated to have it end. The only good thing about going back to school was that Lydia Thompson, my best friend, would be going with me. This was the first summer we'd been apart since fourth grade—Lydia had gone to Camp Mattaquan up in Massachusetts, and I really missed her a lot. She'd come home a week ago, but Mr. and Mrs. Thompson had immediately whisked Lydia and her brother off to New London to visit their grandparents, so I hadn't had a chance to see her yet.

I leaned down and patted Lucky's glossy brown neck.

"I'm going to miss you, too," I told him. "I'm going to miss every single horse at The Barn, and Matthew, and the dogs. I'll probably even miss Zach—but not very much."

Zach Wallace had been working part-time for my uncle for two years, ever since he was my age. He never let me forget that since his father's death, he *had* to work, while I didn't really need the money Matthew paid me—I just did it for fun. Zach always treated me like some dumb little kid who didn't know the first thing about horses. That made me mad, because I was as good a rider as he was—well, almost—and this summer I had worked every bit as hard.

Lucky flicked his ears back and forth as though he was listening to every word I said, but I suspected he was just bothered by the gnats that hovered around his head. They were beginning to get to me, too, so I tugged gently on the reins, turning Lucky up the narrow dirt road that would take us back to The Barn. He picked up his pace right away.

"Maybe it won't be so bad, though," I went on. "If I can just talk Mom and Dad into letting me come out here on weekends and after school sometimes . . ."

It was a pretty big *if*. My parents weren't exactly thrilled that I was a horse nut. It wasn't that they had anything against horses—they just felt I should be developing some other interests, now that I was about to start my sophomore year in high school. But when I had begged to spend my summer vacation working for Matthew at The Barn, they had agreed to let me do it. I guess they thought that after I'd been mucking out stalls and doing all the other dirty work around the stable for a couple of months, I'd be thoroughly sick of horses. Needless to say, that's not what happened.

"I know it won't be easy," I said to Lucky, "but I'm going to give it my best shot. I'll ask them tonight. Who knows? If you're *really* lucky, maybe some of it will rub off on me!"

We were in sight of The Barn now, and though Lucky was eager to get back to his stall, I pulled on the reins until he reluctantly slowed to a stop at the top of a little hill. I loved the view from this particular spot. I could see my uncle's property stretched out below me—the paddocks, the pond where water birds nested and fed, and The Barn itself, bright red against the rock-strewn fields and low green mountains.

Though Matthew owned fifteen horses, which he rented to riders, and boarded nine more, he certainly wasn't rich, and his place wasn't elegant or fancy like some of the horse farms in Litchfield County. He called his stable The Barn because that's what it was, just a big old barn with two cupolas on top and a stable yard in front surrounded by a split-rail fence.

Matthew lived in a hundred-year-old farmhouse nearby. My mom said that he'd ruined the house by putting up those funny-looking panels on the roof. But I thought it was neat that he used solar energy for heat and hot water and grew most of his food in his vegetable garden and orchard. Matthew's my godfather as well as my uncle, and we've always been very close. We're also very much alike: We're both crazy about horses, and we both believe that people shouldn't use up the earth's resources and pollute the environment, because if we don't take care of our planet, who will?

A lot of people in Stockton thought Matthew was kind of weird because of the way he lived, and that includes my mother and father and my older sister, Sabrina. My father had been trying for years to convince Matthew to sell The Barn and accept a partnership in the family business, Sherrill's Department Store. I know he worried about Matthew being financially secure. But Matthew always refused, politely but firmly. Though he had a hard time making ends meet, Matthew loved his work, went his own way, and did his own thing. I really admired him for that, but my parents and Sabrina simply couldn't understand it.

Lucky had been very patient while I sat there admiring the view, but now he started chomping on his bit and pawing the ground. So I gave him his head, and he didn't need any urging to break into a brisk trot. I posted as evenly as possible, considering that he had a pretty rough gait.

As we started down the lane that led to the stable, I could see my tall, rangy uncle talking to a short, stocky, fair-haired man in the stable yard. A small horse trailer was parked behind Zach's beat-up old Chevy outside the fence. *Probably another boarder*, I thought.

Matthew's two German shepherds, Nemo and Flash, were sitting on either side of him like two big bookends. Suddenly Nemo stood up, and the stranger nervously backed away a few paces. I guess he thought Nemo was going to bite him or something. That made me grin, because even though Matthew's dogs look awfully fierce, they're as gentle as a pair of lambs.

As I rode into the stable yard and slid out of the saddle, Matthew looked up and waved, a smile on his bearded face. Flash and Nemo came romping over to Lucky and me, tails wagging and tongues hanging out.

"Hi, guys," I said, patting them and being careful to pay equal attention to both dogs. "Glad to see you, too!"

Flash raced off and came back a moment later with a big stick in her jaws. She dropped it at my feet, looking up at me hopefully. Laughing, I picked it up and threw it as far as I could. I don't have any pets at home—Daddy's allergic to cats, and Mom says dogs are too much trouble—so I loved playing with Nemo and Flash.

As both dogs galloped after the stick, I led Lucky over to Matthew and the other man.

"Good ride, Tess?" my uncle asked, and I nodded. "This is my niece, Theresa Sherrill," he said to the stranger, then turned back to me. "Mr. Graham is going to be boarding his wife's mare with us for a little while."

"Just until we get settled in our new home," Mr. Graham said. "We're moving to New Jersey tomorrow. As soon as we find a stable where we can board her, I'll send somebody to pick up Goldie. Shouldn't be more than a couple of weeks, three at the most."

Matthew smiled. "No problem. Are you sure you don't want to take a look around so you can assure your wife that Goldie will be well taken care of?"

"I'd be glad to give you a quick tour," I added.

Mr. Graham shook his head impatiently, glancing

7

at his watch. "No, no, that won't be necessary. This place has a fine reputation around Stockton. Let's just unload the horse and I'll be on my way."

While he and Matthew headed for the trailer, I quickly led Lucky to his stall. "Back in a minute, boy," I promised, loosening the girth of his saddle. "I want to see what our new boarder looks like."

I hurried back outside—and ran smack into Zach, who was on his way in. He staggered backward, pretending that I had almost knocked him over. As if I could! Zach's about a foot taller than I and probably outweighs me by at least fifty pounds.

"Where's the fire, pipsqueak?" he asked, grinning down at me.

I was tempted to stick out my tongue at him, but that would only have made him tease me more. Instead I said, "Matthew's getting a new boarder. Her name's Goldie, and I want to take a look at her."

Zach followed me. I had just taken off my riding hat, and now I felt him give my long ponytail a tweak. Glancing over my shoulder, I glared at him. "Cut that out!" I said irritably. Honestly, sometimes he acted like he was six years old instead of sixteen.

Still grinning, Zach said, "I just thought I'd do you a favor by wringing it out. Your hair's soaking wet."

"Yours would be too if you had as much of it as I do tucked up under this darned helmet." I slung the hat over my arm by the chin strap, walking faster.

And then I stopped short and gave a little gasp. This time Zach ran into *me*, but I hardly even noticed. I was too busy staring at the mare Matthew was leading into the stable yard.

She was the most beautiful horse I had ever seen. She couldn't have been more than fifteen hands high, and she really *was* golden, with a mane and tail that shone like spun silver. Her head was small and perfectly formed, like an Arabian's. There was a white star on her forehead, and as she picked her way delicately across the ground, I saw that she had four gleaming white socks. Gazing at her, I had the strangest feeling, as if I'd seen her somewhere before.

"Ariel!" I murmured suddenly.

Now I knew why the mare seemed so familiar. I had a collection of model horses at home—they filled an entire bookshelf in my bedroom. I loved them all, but my absolute, all-time favorite was the first one I ever got, the exquisite little palomino that Matthew had given me for my eighth birthday. He had told me her name was Ariel. We had all sorts of wonderful imaginary adventures together, and I dreamed of someday having a real horse of my own that looked exactly like her. Of course, I hadn't played with the model in years—I was much too grown up for that—but I had never forgotten my dream.

As I walked slowly over to the living, breathing mare, I simply couldn't believe my eyes. She looked *exactly* like my model, right down to the star on her forehead and the four white socks!

"I thought you said her name was Goldie," Zach said, coming up beside me and giving the horse a friendly pat.

I didn't bother trying to explain, because I was sure he'd laugh. But Matthew understood. "Amazing resemblance, isn't it, Tess?" he said, smiling. "But I'm afraid she won't fit on one of your shelves."

"Huh?" Zach looked really confused, and I couldn't blame him.

"Her name *is* Goldie," Mr. Graham said. He had joined us after dumping a saddle and bridle on the bench outside the tack-room door. "Golden Dawn, actually, but we call her Goldie for short." He reached into his hip pocket and pulled out a wallet. "Mr. Sherrill, if you'll just tell me how much three weeks' board will be, I'll pay in advance." Taking a credit card out of the wallet, he added, "You *do* take plastic, don't you?"

Matthew shook his head regretfully. "Sorry—cash or check only. My business is too small for me to bother with all that paperwork."

"Drat!" Mr. Graham frowned. "I thought everybody took credit cards these days. I don't have much cash on me, and I left my checkbook at home. Now what do I do?"

"No problem," my uncle said. "If you'll come into the office with me, I'll make out a bill. Take it with you and drop a check in the mail."

Mr. Graham looked surprised. "You'd trust me to do that?"

10

Matthew shrugged. "Why not? I'm an honest man, and I assume you are too." Handing me the lead attached to the palomino's halter, he said, "Tess, why don't you and Zach show this young lady to her new quarters while Mr. Graham and I take care of business? You can put her in the loose box next to Cinnamon's stall." A loose box is a bigger stall, where the horse doesn't have to be tied up.

The two men headed for the little cubicle off the tack room that Matthew used for his office. As soon as they were out of earshot, Zach said, "If you ask me, Matthew's *too* trusting. I mean, what does he know about that guy? He's leaving town in a couple of days—what if he never pays up?"

I heard Zach's words, but they didn't really register. I was still too overcome by the sudden appearance of my dream horse to think about anything else. Even when Ariel—I just couldn't think of her by any other name—gently nudged me with her nose, I couldn't quite believe it.

And then she took a step forward and planted one dainty hoof squarely on my foot.

"Ouch!" I squawked, giggling. It didn't really hurt all that much because I was wearing boots, and she stepped off immediately, but it was enough to convince me that she was real, all right. I threw my arms around her silky golden neck and buried my face in her mane for a moment, breathing in the wonderful warm, horsey scent of her.

11

"Are you coming, or what?" Zach asked. "We still have to do evening feed, you know."

I beamed at him. "I know," I said. "We're coming, aren't we, Ariel?"

As we walked toward the stable entrance, Zach said, "Why do you keep calling her Ariel when her name's Goldie?"

I decided I might as well tell him, whether he laughed at me or not. "Years ago Matthew gave me a model horse that looks just like her, and he told me its name was Ariel. When I was older, I discovered that he'd named the model after a character in Shakespeare's play *The Tempest*."

"Oh yeah," Zach said. "I remember *The Tempest*. We studied it in English last year. That's the one about the crazy old magician that lives on a desert island, and his daughter falls in love with a ship-wrecked sailor, right? And Ariel's like a good fairy, and Caliban's the bad guy."

I smiled. "That's the one. You really know your Shakespeare."

"Well, English is my best subject," Zach told me.

"Really? Mine too." I was surprised. Somehow I'd never pictured Zach being interested in any academic subject, and certainly not English. I guess that's because he and his mother live on a farm and Zach goes to the Consolidated School instead of Stockton High, like Sabrina and me. I kind of took it for granted that farm kids learned only about things like cattle raising and crop rotation and stuff. It had never occurred to me that Zach might actually have studied Shakespeare and, what's more, enjoyed it. I realized then that I didn't know very much about Zach at all, even though we'd spent the whole summer working together.

"I guess it wouldn't hurt to call her Ariel as long as she's here," Zach said as we walked into the stable. "She can go back to being Golden Dawn when Mr. Graham picks her up."

All the horses heard the *clop, clop* of the palomino's hooves on the plank floor. They poked their heads over their stall doors to check out the newcomer, and when I saw Lucky, still wearing his saddle and bridle, I felt guilty. I stopped in front of his stall and stroked his nose.

"I'll take off your tack and rub you down real soon," I told him. "But first there's somebody I want you to meet."

Ariel was right behind me, and now she stretched out her neck and touched noses with Lucky. He flicked his ears a couple of times, then gave a little snort and turned away to munch on a few shreds of hay. Obviously he wasn't very impressed, but nothing ever impressed Lucky much unless it had something to do with food.

We continued down the aisle between the stalls to the loose box Matthew had mentioned. Zach was already there, holding the door open. I led the palomino inside, glad that just the other day Zach and I had cleaned the empty stall and spread fresh,

13

sweet-smelling straw on the floor. *Nothing but the best will do for Ariel,* I thought as I unlatched the lead line from her halter.

I wished I hadn't fed all the carrots and apples I'd brought with me that morning to the other horses. I wanted to give the mare a special treat to welcome her to The Barn. Putting my hand into the pocket of my jeans, I discovered only one sticky, slightly furry mint. It wasn't exactly what I had in mind, but it was better than nothing. I held the mint out to Ariel on the palm of my outstretched hand. She sniffed at it— her warm breath tickled—and then she took it, her lips soft as velvet against my skin.

"Pretty good-looking horse," Zach said as we went out of the stall and closed the door behind us. "Kinda small, though. If I rode her, I bet my feet would almost touch the ground." He glanced over at me. "But she'd be perfect for you, pipsqueak. Too bad you won't be coming to The Barn much anymore."

"Who said I wouldn't be? Sorry, Zach, but you might not get rid of me so soon. I've decided to try to convince my folks to let me keep coming here after school or on weekends, if it's okay with Matthew."

"Hey, that's great," Zach said, to my surprise. "If you left, I wouldn't have anybody to tease. Matthew's terrific, and I really like working for him, but you gotta admit Orville's not a whole lot of fun."

That was the understatement of the year. Orville

14

Cartwright, my uncle's full-time stable hand, was a lanky, sour-faced New Englander who could have been anywhere between forty and sixty-five. He never spoke unless you asked him a question, and then all he usually said was "Yep" or "Nope."

"So what about evening feed?" Zach asked now.

"You start," I said, still gazing at Ariel. "As soon as I take off Lucky's tack, I'll help you."

"Well, make it snappy. I told Mom I'd be home for dinner by six, and it's almost five thirty." Zach started clumping toward the feed room, and after one last, lingering look at the palomino mare, I followed him, heading for Lucky's stall.

But I couldn't help glancing over my shoulder to see if Ariel was watching me. She was. She stuck her lovely little head out over the door of the loose box, following me with her big brown eyes. I thought she looked awfully sad, as if she couldn't understand why her owners had abandoned her or why the people who had put her in this strange place had left her all alone.

I ran back and gave her a hug. "It's okay, Ariel," I said. "I guess you're homesick, and I don't blame you. But Matthew will take good care of you, and I'll visit you every chance I get. You're going to like it here, honest."

The mare snorted softly, as if to say she doubted it.

"Really, you will," I murmured, running my fingers through her silvery mane. "Don't worry, and please don't be sad. I'll bring you treats whenever I

15

can, and we'll go on rides together. It'll be great. You'll see."

"Hey, pipsqueak, get a move on!" Zach yelled.

"I'll be right there, Zach. Calm down!" Then I kissed Ariel's velvety nose. "I'll come back to see you just as soon as I can," I promised her.

Until now, being able to ride Lucky had been enough to make me want to keep coming to The Barn. But the chance of getting to know—and maybe even *riding*—the palomino made me twice as determined. Even though the mare belonged to Mr. and Mrs. Graham, I thought of her as *my* horse, the horse I'd been dreaming of since I was eight years old. For the few weeks she would be staying at Matthew's stable, I wanted to spend every minute I could with her. And when the Grahams took her away—well, I couldn't even bear to think about it.

¬2¬

Zach and I finished our stable chores in record time. Even so, I would have missed the last bus to town if Fred the driver hadn't waited while I dashed up the dirt road to Route 22. Fred and I had become pals over the summer, and he knew my schedule pretty well by now. Once we got to Stockton, he even made a special stop at the corner of Brookfield and Willow streets so I had to walk only half a block to my house.

"Guess I won't be seeing you much anymore, what with school starting and all," Fred said as he pulled over to the curb that evening. "You're not going to have a whole lot of time for horsing around."

He laughed at his own joke, and I laughed too.

17

"Oh, I don't know," I said. "You might see me pretty soon."

The door whooshed open and I stepped out, waving to Fred as the bus drove away. Then I started walking along the peaceful, tree-lined street toward home.

I was half a block away from my house before I noticed the little dark-green sports car parked by the curb. *Drat!* I thought, scowling. The car belonged to Sabrina's boyfriend, Edward Brewster, and it meant that Edward would probably be staying for supper.

It wasn't that I didn't like Edward (nobody ever called him Ed or Eddie). He was handsome, charming, and polite to everybody, even me, which hadn't always been true of my sister's other boyfriends. But somehow he seemed almost *too* polite, too perfect, to be real.

Maybe that was because he was older than the guys Sabrina used to date. She was a senior at Stockton High, but Edward had just begun his sophomore year at Whitfield College here in town, and his father was a very successful real-estate developer. Sabrina and our parents thought Edward was terribly mature because he had his future all mapped out. As soon as he graduated from college, he was going into partnership with Mr. Brewster, building shopping malls and stuff like that all over Connecticut. I didn't approve of that at all. I mean, we really *need* more shopping malls messing up the countryside and fouling up the environment, right?

18

But that wasn't why I was annoyed to see his car. If Edward was there, I wouldn't be able to tackle my folks right away about working for Matthew once school began. That meant that I'd have to wait until after Edward left to talk to them about it, and who knew how long he might stay?

Frowning, I opened the front door.

"Oh, hello, sweetie," my mother said as I came into the hall. Even though she was carrying a big bowl of chicken parts, she looked as beautiful and elegant as ever, in beige slacks and a silk shirt that almost exactly matched her soft blond hair.

Everybody says that my mom looks much too young to have two teenage daughters, and they're right. Everybody also says that she and Sabrina look more like sisters than mother and daughter, and they're right about that, too. Though Sabrina inherited our father's height, she has the same fair hair and peaches-and-cream complexion as Mom. I'm just the opposite. I'm dark, like Dad and Matthew, and short, like Mom—"petite," she calls it.

"We're barbecuing on the terrace tonight," my mother said now. "Your father wants to take advantage of the good weather while it lasts."

"You mean Dad's actually home?" I said, surprised and delighted. "That's great!"

I guess you'd call my father a workaholic. He often went to his office seven days a week, catching up with paperwork on Sundays when the store was closed.

Smiling, Mom said, "I managed to convince him that Sherrill's won't fall apart if the president takes an occasional evening off." Then her smile faded. "If only Matthew . . ."

She didn't finish the sentence. She didn't have to— I knew what she was thinking, because I'd heard it so many times before: "If only Matthew would give up this stable nonsense and share the responsibility of running the store, your father wouldn't have to work so hard."

I hated it when my mother talked about my uncle that way. It made me feel guilty for enjoying The Barn so much, as if I was taking Matthew's side against my parents in their constant struggle to make him behave more conventionally. And I wasn't, not really. I loved my parents, but I loved Matthew, too, and I just wished my mom and dad would stop trying to turn him into somebody he wasn't.

Mom knew how I felt about the whole thing, which must have been why she quickly changed the subject. "Edward's here—you must have seen his car outside."

I nodded.

"Sabrina has invited him to stay for supper. So run upstairs and make yourself presentable, dear. And *don't* forget to take off your boots before you do. I don't want you tracking stable dirt through the house." My mother is head decorator at Sherrill's, so of course she likes our house to be as spotless as the Home Decorating Department at the store.

I pulled off my boots and ran up the stairs in my stocking feet. I showered as fast as I could and changed into a pair of baggy white shorts and a blue chambray shirt, tossing the grubby T-shirt and jeans I'd been wearing into the laundry hamper.

As I was combing my hair in front of my dresser, I noticed my collection of miniature horses reflected in the mirror. Putting down my comb, I went over to where the palomino stood between the dapple-gray Arabian and the prancing black stallion. I picked up Ariel and gazed at her. It was amazing! The mare Mr. Graham called Goldie had the exact same markings as my miniature. It hadn't just been my imagination. But it was still hard to believe that only an hour ago I had thrown my arms around the neck of Ariel's exact duplicate in the flesh.

Then and there I decided that, Edward or no Edward, I was going to talk to my parents as soon as possible about working at The Barn this fall. I carefully returned the palomino to her place. I was just starting to fasten my hair with a barrette when I heard someone tapping at my bedroom door.

"Get a move on, Tess," my sister called. "The chicken's almost ready."

"I'll be right there," I called back.

I finished fixing my hair, slipped my feet into my favorite beat-up leather sandals, and hurried downstairs.

A few minutes later, when I paused in the open doorway that led to the terrace, I saw Sabrina sitting in a lawn chair next to Edward, sipping a tall iced tea and listening with rapt attention to whatever he was saying. She was wearing a turquoise tank top and baggy white shorts just like mine, but they looked a lot better on her because she has incredibly long, slim legs.

Edward, handsome as ever in an immaculate white polo shirt and perfectly pressed chinos, reminded me of one of the mannequins in the men's department at Sherrill's, but I had to admit that he and my sister made a very good-looking couple.

Mom was also listening intently to Edward as she offered him a platter of fresh vegetables arranged around a bowl of dip.

"My father's really excited about it," Edward was saying. He selected a bright green bean and dunked it into the dip. "It'll be the finest residential development in Connecticut. He's going to call it Brewster Estates."

"That's wonderful news," my mother said.

"It certainly is," my father added from behind the grill. "This just might make a major difference to our family."

I couldn't figure out how one of Mr. Brewster's boring real-estate deals could affect us at all, but I didn't waste any time thinking about it. The chicken smelled delicious, and I suddenly realized how hungry I was.

As I came out onto the terrace, my father smiled

warmly at me. "There's my girl!" he said. "Where have you been all this time?"

I ran over to him and stood on tiptoe to kiss his cheek. "Just getting ready," I told him. "I'm starving, Dad. When do we eat?"

He poked at a piece of chicken with his long fork. "In about fifteen minutes. I need a little more barbecue sauce."

I brought the bowl of sauce and the brush to him from the umbrella table. "Why don't you let me keep an eye on the grill while you relax?" I suggested.

"Thanks, honey. I think I'll take you up on that."

He sank into a chair next to Sabrina's, and my mother poured him a tall, frosty glass of lemonade. My parents looked happy and relaxed, and I decided this might be the time to bring up the subject of The Barn.

Daddy gave me the perfect opening. "How were the trails today, Tess?" he asked. "Must have been busy for the holiday."

"Oh, yes," I told him. "It was a great day. And Matthew got a new boarder this afternoon, a beautiful palomino mare. Her owners are moving out of state. They're only leaving her with Matthew until they get settled in their new place, so she won't be staying for very long. There's a problem, though," I added, brushing barbecue sauce on the nearest piece of chicken. "Someone will have to exercise her while she's there, and she's pretty small, probably not even fifteen hands."

"I think that's very interesting," Edward said seriously. "That horses are measured in hands, but people are measured in feet. I wonder why that is?"

I shrugged. "Beats me. They just are. Anyway, this mare—I call her Ariel—isn't very big, and neither am I. But Matthew and Zach are. Big, I mean." I took a deep breath and said all in a rush, "So I was wondering if maybe I could go out and ride her every now and then because it might not be good for her to be ridden all the time by people who are too heavy."

There! I'd done it! I hadn't known exactly what I was going to say until I'd said it. And I hate to admit it, but it wasn't exactly true that Ariel ought to have a light rider. I didn't think my parents would know that, though. Suddenly I realized that I'd been basting the same chicken leg for about five minutes, so I quickly began slapping some sauce on the other parts while I waited anxiously to hear what my parents had to say.

Mom and Dad looked at each other. It was one of those looks that take the place of discussion. They've been married so long that they each know what the other is thinking without either of them saying a single word.

At last my father said, "I don't suppose it would do any harm," at the same time my mother said, "I don't see why not."

I could hardly believe my ears. I'd been gearing up for a major battle, and they'd said yes right away!

"You mean it?" I cried. "I can keep going out to The Barn?"

My father nodded. "Certainly not the first week of school, but occasionally. And if there's the slightest indication that you're neglecting your studies, Tess . . ."

"Oh, I won't, I promise!" I ran over and gave him and my mother each a big hug. "Thanks! This is so great! I was afraid I'd never see Ariel again."

"I thought you said the horse only arrived this afternoon," Sabrina said. She sounded puzzled. "How come you're so attached to it all of a sudden?"

"It's not really so sudden. Remember that model palomino Matthew gave me a long time ago, the one that started my collection? Well, this mare . . ." I broke off, knowing that my sister, who didn't care at all about horses, wouldn't understand. So I simply said, "She reminds me of the model."

"That's nice, dear," my mother said. "It's just as well that she'll only be boarding with your uncle for a little while. From what Edward was saying right before you joined us, it seems that Matthew may be closing The Barn fairly soon."

For the second time in less than five minutes, I wasn't sure I'd heard right. Only this time it wasn't a pleasant surprise. I stared at her in astonishment. "Close The Barn?" I gasped. "Why? What do you mean?"

Sabrina turned to Edward. "Maybe you'd better fill Tess in on Brewster Estates."

"There's not a whole lot to tell," he said, giving me one of his most charming smiles. "Dad's planning on building a luxury residential community outside of town, and he's approached Eli Putnam about buying his land. Mr. Putnam's really eager to sell."

I wasn't surprised. I'd never been able to figure out how Old Man Putnam and his two sons were able to make a living on their run-down farm next to my uncle's property. If he wanted to sell, it made a lot of sense, though I wasn't crazy about the idea of a residential development so close to Matthew's land, no matter how luxurious it was. I was sure that Matthew wouldn't be either. But what did that have to do with his closing The Barn?

Edward told me. "Dad wants Mr. Sherrill's property to complete the parcel. He'll be out of town for a while, but he's planning on making your uncle a very attractive offer as soon as he gets back—almost twice what a farm that size is worth in today's market. It's a terrific deal. The way I see it, Mr. Sherrill can't possibly refuse."

"This may be just the incentive Matthew needs to get his act together and be more responsible with his finances and his future," Daddy said. He leaned back in his chair and took a sip of his lemonade. "Once he understands how much his land is worth to Mr. Brewster, he's bound to realize that this horse nonsense isn't going to support him in his old age."

"How Matthew has managed to break even all

26

these years is a mystery to me," my mother added. "And when he sells, your father intends to offer him a full partnership in the store, as he has so often before. But this time we think Matthew will accept."

You might think I'd be very upset by what I'd just heard, but I wasn't. In fact, I was relieved! I'd been afraid something awful had happened that would force Matthew to close The Barn, but it hadn't. Nothing had happened at all. Though everybody else took it for granted that he'd sell his property to Mr. Brewster, I knew my uncle better than that, and I was absolutely positive they were wrong. He loved his horses and his land, and there wasn't enough money in the world to make him give them up. But I didn't say anything. I just listened.

"It'll be so nice to finally have an uncle who has a normal job," Sabrina said. "Remember last fall, when Matthew made such a fuss and reported old Josiah Talley to the SPCA for horse abuse? It was actually on the front page of the Stockton *Times*! My whole class was talking about it. I was so embarrassed!"

Daddy nodded. "I remember. Josiah used to be one of the store's best customers. After that, he never set foot in Sherrill's again."

"Mr. Talley hasn't set foot in *any* store for the past couple of months," I pointed out. "He died in July!"

"We know that, Tess," Mom said. "But his daughter Joanna hasn't come by either. I'm afraid she bears our family a grudge. From what I hear, Mr.

Talley didn't leave her very well off, and she's been having a difficult time building up her new boarding business. Nobody will trust her with their horses because of Matthew's accusations."

I guess I should have shut up, considering that everything had gone my way so far, but I couldn't help rushing to my uncle's defense. "They weren't just accusations, Mom," I said. "The SPCA investigation proved they were true."

"We know that, Tess," my father said. "All we're saying is that Matthew could have handled the whole affair with a little more tact, considering . . ."

"Excuse me, Mr. Sherrill," Edward interrupted politely, "but I believe the chicken's burning."

"Oh my gosh!" I exclaimed. "I forgot all about it!" Truthfully, I was thankful for the interruption. I didn't want to argue with my parents just now, and I had been about to.

I raced my father to the grill, but he got there first. Snatching up the fork, he quickly began turning the half-charred pieces over. Fortunately he was still in a good mood. "It's all right," he said cheerfully. "I like my chicken well done. Sabrina, why don't you help your mother bring out the rest of the food? I think it's time to eat."

Was it ever! I was so hungry that anything would have tasted good, even charcoal chicken. My mother and Sabrina went into the house and came back with a big tossed salad and a kind of weird-looking loaf of bread that my sister proudly announced she had baked herself. It wasn't nearly as bad as it looked, though. Edward was very impressed, and so was I— Sabrina wasn't exactly what you'd call the domestic type.

I was glad when the conversation turned from Brewster Estates to other topics. There was a lot of talk about what colleges Sabrina would be applying to, and then she and Mom suddenly zeroed in on me. They both seemed to think that since I was entering tenth grade, it was time I changed my image. I didn't know I had one, but according to them, I'd become scruffy looking from hanging out with the horses all summer, and they were afraid I'd stay that way once I was back in school.

"After all, Tess, you'll be fifteen next month," Sabrina said, munching on a blackened chicken leg. "You really ought to start dressing—and smelling— like a girl, instead of a grubby stable hand."

"Now wait a minute!" I said, frowning at her. "I take as many showers as you do. Besides, I *like* the smell of horses."

"That's fine, dear," my mother said. "But that doesn't mean you should dress for school the same way you dress for the stables. I hope you won't let all those new clothes we bought last week hang unused in the closet."

I didn't see what was wrong with my good old jeans and boots, but I didn't want to rock the boat.

29

Right now I just shrugged and said, "Don't worry, Mom. I'll wear my new clothes." I would have been willing to wear nothing but ruffles and lace if it meant I'd be able to spend time with Ariel!

~3~

Lydia stopped by my house the next morning so we could walk to school together. We were so happy to see each other that we hugged and squealed and jumped up and down like a couple of little kids.

When we finally calmed down, I stepped back and stared at my best friend, who was dressed in a bright tropical-print shirt that set off her dark tan, and a short, acid-green skirt. "You look fantastic," I cried. "But you look so *different*! You've bleached your hair, and you're wearing glasses, and you've *grown*!"

Laughing, Lydia tossed her head, making her thick, blond-streaked brown hair swirl around her shoulders. "You're nuts," she said. "In the first place, I haven't grown. I'm still five seven, but I'm wearing these great wedgies I found in a thrift shop in New

31

London." She stuck out one foot so I could admire the lemon-yellow shoe. "In the second place, I didn't bleach my hair—the sun did. And in the third place, I lost one of my contacts the first week of camp so I had to wear my glasses. I thought I told you about it in one of my letters."

I made a face at her. "Which one? The one you sent right after you got there, or the one you sent right before you left?"

Lydia looked distressed for a moment. "Did I really only write to you twice? Gee, Tess, I'm sorry. I meant to write every day, but you know how it is. You didn't write to me very often, either, you fink! Anyway, I got used to my glasses so I decided to keep wearing them. The tortoiseshell frames make me look like a real reporter, don't you think?" she asked, widening her big green eyes, which appeared even bigger and greener behind the lenses. "That's going to be the topic of my first column in the *Advocate*—'Contacts Aren't Cool: Glasses Are Glamorous.' " Lydia wrote the fashion column for the school paper. Now she peered at me. "You've changed too. As a matter of fact, you look terrific! I love your skirt, and that purple top looks great on you. Straight from the racks of Sherrill's Junior Scene, right?" I nodded. "What happened? Did Sabrina burn all your ratty jeans?"

I laughed. "No, but she wanted to. She and my mom were on my back about dressing like a stable hand. I decided to try and look nice, because . . ."

32

As we walked down Brookfield Street, I told Lydia everything that had happened the day before. Though she wasn't horse crazy like me—I'd been able to drag her out to The Barn only a couple of times, and that was years ago—she understood exactly how I felt about Ariel and everything else, just as I knew she would.

"It's too bad the palomino won't be around for very long," she said when I had finished. "But I'm sure you're right. Your uncle would never sell The Barn and become a department store executive. And even after Ariel leaves, maybe your folks will let you keep riding his other horses. I *did* tell you in one of those letters that I took riding at camp, didn't I? It was a great way to meet cute guys. I only fell off twice, and each time, the most gorgeous boy helped me get back into the saddle." Linking her arm through mine, Lydia went on, "Of course, I didn't have a real boyfriend, but I plan to find one now that school is starting."

"Oh, no! Then you'll be as boring as Sabrina. She used to be a lot of fun, before she fell in love the first time—and the second time, and the third time. Each time was worse than the last. Now just about all she thinks or talks about is Edward Brewster."

"Cross my heart and hope to die, I promise I will *not* become boring," Lydia said solemnly, "even if I fall madly in love. And you have to promise me the same thing."

I laughed. "No problem! As far as I'm concerned,

33

horses are a lot more interesting than boys. And speaking of horses, how about coming out to The Barn with me on Saturday? I can't wait for you to meet Ariel."

"Sure, why not?" Lydia said. "After all you've told me about her, I can't wait to meet her either."

I was sure that the first week of school would seem endless. But though I thought about the palomino constantly, there was so much to do that the days passed quickly, and almost before I knew it, it was Saturday.

I'd set my alarm, but I woke up long before it went off and put on a baggy sweatshirt and my most comfortable old jeans. I tiptoed downstairs to the kitchen in my stocking feet, carrying my boots so I wouldn't wake anybody else. I was much too excited to eat real food, so I threw orange juice, a banana, and some yogurt into the blender and whipped up my favorite "no-breakfast" breakfast.

Then I made a couple of sandwiches for Lydia and me to eat for lunch, cut up a lot of carrots and apples to bring to Ariel and the other horses, and watched the clock until it was time to meet Lydia at the bus stop. I hoped she wouldn't be late. If we missed the nine o'clock bus, there wouldn't be another one until ten, and that would cut a whole hour out of my precious day.

Fortunately Lydia got there right on time, looking as if she'd just stepped out of one of those catalogues of expensive riding clothes, in tan stretch pants, shiny brown boots, and a pale-blue cotton sweater. I guess I looked pretty grungy by comparison, but I didn't care. After making such an effort to look nice all week, I felt like myself again, and it was a very good feeling. Fred greeted me warmly as we boarded the bus. I introduced him to Lydia, and we took our seats.

About twenty minutes later, Lydia and I were tramping down the dirt road to The Barn. Matthew was just coming out of his office, with Nemo and Flash at his heels. His bearded face lit up with a broad smile, and the dogs raced over to us, almost knocking me down in their eagerness to welcome me.

Lydia backed away nervously. "It's okay," I shouted over the dogs' frantic barking. "Don't be scared—these guys wouldn't hurt a fly."

"What about a *person*?" Lydia said, staggering a little as Nemo leaped up, planted his paws on her chest, and began licking her face. "Nice doggie. *Down*, doggie! Tess, *help!*"

"Nemo! Flash!" Matthew called sternly. "Come! Sit! Stay!"

They came, sat, and stayed while Matthew strode over to Lydia and me. "Hi, stranger," he said, putting an arm around my shoulders. "I've really missed you this past week, and so have the horses."

I grinned at him. "I've missed all of you, too. It's so good to be back!"

Glancing at Lydia, Matthew said, "I see you've brought reinforcements. Who's this?"

"Lydia Thompson, my best friend," I told him. "You met her a long time ago, but she's changed a lot since then."

Matthew shook Lydia's hand vigorously. "Hello, Lydia. Welcome to The Barn."

"Hi, Mr. Sherrill," Lydia said, smiling. "Tess has been telling me about this special horse that's boarding here, the palomino. I came especially to meet her."

"Call me Matthew," my uncle said. "As for Ariel, you can meet her right now. There she is."

Sure enough, Zach was leading the mare into the stable yard. In the bright morning sunlight, her coat gleamed like pure gold.

I clutched Lydia's arm. "Doesn't she look exactly like my model? Isn't she gorgeous?"

"He sure is!" Lydia breathed.

It took me a couple of seconds to realize that she hadn't made a mistake. Lydia wasn't looking at Ariel. She was gazing at Zach with stars in her eyes.

"*This* is the guy you were working with all summer?" she asked. "The one you complained about in your few letters?"

I shrugged. "That's him. Zach Wallace. I guess he's not really all that bad, but he can be a real pain in the neck sometimes."

"Wow!" Lydia whispered. "There were a lot of

foxy guys at camp, but compared to Zach—well, there's just no comparison."

"Give me a break," I groaned. "Camp Mattaquan must have softened your brain!"

With Lydia close behind, I hurried over to the trough, where Zach was letting Ariel have a drink. The minute she saw me, she raised her head and whickered, as if she actually remembered me.

"Hi, pipsqueak," Zach said in his usual annoying fashion.

"Hi, Zach. How's it going?" I replied, but I wasn't looking at him. I couldn't take my eyes off Ariel. I stroked her gently, murmuring how glad I was to see her.

Lydia poked me in the ribs. *"Tess!"* she hissed. "Introduce me!"

I knew she wasn't talking about the mare. Reluctantly I tore my attention away from Ariel. "Lydia Thompson, this is Zachary Wallace. Zach, this is my best friend, Lydia."

"Tess has told me so much about you," Lydia said, beaming at him.

"I bet she has." Zach glanced at me with a wry grin. "I plead not guilty—to most of it, anyway."

"Oh, she didn't say anything bad," Lydia said. "And she sure didn't tell me you were so—"

"Tall," I cut in, before she could finish. Lydia has this way of blurting out exactly what she's thinking, and sometimes that's okay. But other times, like now, I had to save her from making a total fool of

herself. "So how's Ariel doing?" I asked Zach. "Is she still homesick? Has she been eating all right? Who's been exercising her?"

Zach laughed. "Hey, what is this—twenty questions? She's doing fine. If she's homesick, I haven't noticed. She's been eating okay, and Matthew and I have both been riding her. But now that you're here, you can take over for today. Matthew'll probably let you take her out on a couple of trail rides. That is, unless you and your friend . . ."

"Lydia," Lydia reminded him.

". . . Unless you and Lydia are just going to hang out and goof off."

I glared at him. "No way! I came here to work just like I did all summer, and Lydia's going to work too. Aren't you, Lydia?"

She nodded. "Absolutely!"

Zach glanced at her skeptically. "Yeah? In those fancy clothes?"

"These old things?" Lydia said. "This is what I wore for riding all summer at Camp Mattaquan. Ever hear of it?"

Zach shook his head. "Nope."

"Oh, well, I learned a lot at camp about working at a stable. We had to saddle and bridle our horses and groom them and feed them and everything. You just tell me what to do, and I'll do it."

"Okay, you're on," Zach said. "You can start by helping Orville muck out the stalls. I'll find you a shovel."

The prospect of shoveling manure didn't seem to faze Lydia in the least. She just smiled radiantly, pushed her glasses farther up on the bridge of her nose, and said, "Ready when you are."

Handing Ariel's lead line to me, Zach said, "Here, pipsqueak. I was going to lunge her for a while in the paddock, but if you're thinking of riding her later, you might as well take her back inside for now. Orville's already cleaned her loose box. And then you can give me a hand with the grooming."

He headed for the stable door, Lydia at his side. She hadn't even glanced at the palomino. As they went in, I heard Zach say, "Did they teach you anything about cleaning stalls at that camp?"

"No, but I can learn," my starry-eyed friend replied.

I patted Ariel's glossy golden neck. "Don't feel bad," I told her. "Lydia didn't mean to be rude. It's just that at the moment, she's more interested in Zach than in you. Weird, isn't it?"

Ariel snorted as if she agreed that it was. Then she pricked up her ears and nudged my plastic bag with her nose.

"Oh, I almost forgot!" I exclaimed. "I brought treats for you and Lucky. And for the other horses, of course." I took out a piece of carrot and offered it to her on the palm of my hand. She ate it right away, so I gave her several more, and some apple slices too.

"Hey, Tess! Are you gonna stay out there all day?"

Zach yelled from inside the stable. "I thought you said you came here to work. We have to finish this stuff before the riders start showing up."

I sighed. "He's right," I told Ariel. "I'd better take you in now. It's a beautiful day, and Matthew's bound to have lots of business. But we'll have some good long rides later on."

After I led the palomino to her stall, I said a quick hello to the rest of the horses, giving them each a treat. I visited Lucky's stall last and discovered Lydia there, shoveling away. She didn't see me, and I had to step out of the way fast to avoid being hit by a load of soiled straw as she tossed it over her shoulder and into the wheelbarrow.

"Hey, watch it!" I cried.

Lydia spun around. There were pieces of straw sticking out of her hair, and her boots weren't shiny anymore, but she looked happy. "Sorry about that!" she said with a giggle. "Zach showed me the flip-and-dump technique, but I guess I should have looked before I flipped." She reached out and patted Lucky's rump. "This is such a pretty horse. Chestnut's my favorite horse color."

"Bay," I corrected, giving Lucky a piece of apple. "He's a bay. Chestnuts are reddish brown."

"He *is* reddish brown," Lydia pointed out.

"Yes, but Lucky has a black mane and tail and black socks, so that makes him a bay."

Lydia frowned. "If he's mostly chestnut colored,

why isn't he a chestnut, no matter what color the rest of him is?"

"Lydia, believe me, Lucky is a bay," I said patiently. "That's just the way it is, okay?"

"If you say so. You're the expert." She gave the gelding a push to make him move over, and began shoveling again where he had been standing. "I guess I don't know as much about horses as I thought I did. But once I've been coming out here with you for a while, I'll get it straight. I don't want Zach to think I don't know one end of a horse from the other."

I couldn't help laughing. "After you've mucked out a few more stalls, you won't have any trouble figuring *that* out!" Then I realized what she'd just said. "Do you mean you're going to keep coming to The Barn?"

"I sure am." Lydia dumped another load into the wheelbarrow, more carefully this time. "I want to learn everything you have to teach me, O wise one. Not to mention getting to know a certain tall, handsome stable hand a whole lot better. I mean, since you're not interested, Zach's available, right?"

"Oh, he's available, I guess," I said. "But take it from me, Lydia, you'd have better luck getting his attention if you had four legs and a tail!"

She promptly pawed the ground with one foot and let out a whinny that made Lucky stare at her in amazement. Lydia and I both broke up. We were laughing so hard that Zach, who happened to be passing by, peered at us over the half door.

"What's so funny?" he asked.

"Private joke. You wouldn't understand," I managed to say between giggles.

Zach rolled his eyes. "Well, hurry it up, pipsqueak. Mrs. Bronson just drove up, and she'll be wanting to ride Midnight. Saddle him, will you?"

"Yes, *sir*!" I said, giving him a snappy salute. "Right away, sir!"

For the next hour, we were all so busy that I hardly saw Lydia at all. But the first chance I got, I asked Matthew if it would be okay for me to take Ariel on a couple of trail rides. I was so excited when he said I could. He also said that Lydia should ride Lucky since she wasn't all that experienced, and Lucky was one of the steadiest horses at The Barn. I was glad Lucky was coming along. I didn't want him to feel neglected now that I'd be riding Ariel.

Pretty soon people began arriving for the first trail ride of the day. When Lydia volunteered to collect their money and hand out riding hats while Zach and I got the horses ready, Matthew readily agreed.

Once everybody was mounted, my uncle delivered his standard safety lecture, and we started off. Zach took the lead on Moonshine, his favorite gray gelding, Lydia and Lucky followed close behind, and I brought up the rear on Ariel. When the other riders in the group oohed and aahed over how beautiful she was, it made me feel as proud as if she were my very own horse. In fact, I have to admit that I let them think she was. It was the first time I'd ridden the palomino, and I was thrilled by the smoothness of her gaits and how responsive she was to my lightest touch on the reins.

When we returned to The Barn, Zach, Lydia, and I hardly had time to cool down the horses and eat our sandwiches before another group began to assemble. This time Zach led the trail ride by himself while Lydia and I helped Orville bring in some of the boarders' horses from the north pasture and saddle them so their owners could ride. There was a steady stream of regulars, too, who had been renting horses at The Barn so long that Matthew let them go out without supervision.

"Is it always this busy?" Lydia asked as she put a handful of bills into the cash box. "We must have taken in over four hundred dollars so far, and it's only mid-afternoon."

"As long as the weather's good, The Barn does really well," I said. "But once winter sets in, almost nobody rides at all. For Matthew's sake, I'm hoping it'll be a long, warm autumn."

By the time Zach returned with his group, over a dozen people were waiting for the next trail ride. There were too many for him to handle alone, so I went with him on Ariel, and Lydia tagged along on Lucky.

It was close to four when we got back. The sky was getting cloudy, and a chilly breeze had sprung up, making me shiver. "I guess we won't be getting any more riders today," I said to Orville, who was helping to lead the horses into the stable. He just grunted. "Maybe I'd better find out if Matthew has some more chores for us to do," I went on. "Is he in the office?"

"Nope."

"The tack room?"

"Nope."

I was getting exasperated. "Do you know where he is?"

"Yep."

Gritting my teeth, I said, "Would you mind telling me?"

"Nope." Just as I was about to lose it completely, Orville said, "Went into town 'bout half hour ago." Long pause. "Meeting somebody named Brewster."

There was only one thing Mr. Brewster could be talking to my uncle about, and that was buying Matthew's land. *Well,* I thought, *he's wasting his time, and the sooner he finds that out, the sooner he can start looking around for another location for Brewster Estates.*

"Thanks for the information, Orville," I said.

Orville silently began unsaddling Cinnamon. I had just loosened Frenchie's girth when all of a sudden I heard an incredibly loud roaring noise. Running outside, I saw a bunch of motorcycles coming down the dirt road from Route 22. There were six of them, and as I watched, the cyclists parked their bikes by the stable yard. In their iridescent, brightly colored helmets, goggles, and silver-studded black-leather jackets, they looked like visitors from another planet. They also looked dangerous.

~4~

Zach and Lydia came out of the stable as the bikers strolled into the yard. When they stopped to read The Barn's "Rules, Regulations, and Rates," which were posted on the office door, I could see the word PANTHERS picked out in silver studs on the backs of some of their leather jackets. Lydia hesitated, but Zach strode right over to the guys.

"Looking to rent some horses?" he asked.

"At ten bucks an hour? You gotta be kidding, man," said a beefy biker in a scarlet helmet. "Doncha give group discounts?"

Zach said calmly, "No. That's the going rate."

The scarlet-helmeted biker huddled with his friends for a moment. They all mumbled a lot, and finally the guy turned back to Zach. "Okay. Bring on the nags. Me and my pals wanna ride. And we're not gonna wear any of them hats—we got our helmets.''

Lydia scurried into the office and came back out holding the cash box. "That's ten dollars an hour *each*," she said. "Payment in advance, of course."

As the bikers began handing her their money, I went over to Zach. "Listen," I said very softly so they couldn't hear. "I don't like the looks of these guys. Matthew's not here right now, but I'll bet he wouldn't want them riding his horses."

He glanced down at me with a patronizing smile. "Chill out, okay? They're not Hell's Angels or anything like that—the one in the red helmet probably isn't much older than me. They just act tough because they think it's cool."

"Maybe," I said, but I wasn't convinced, not by a long shot. "I still don't think we should let them ride without Matthew's say-so. Why don't you ask them to wait until he gets back?"

Zach's smile faded, replaced by the stubborn scowl I knew so well. "Who knows when that will be? What am I supposed to do, tell them the boss isn't here right now, and the boss's niece is scared of them?"

"I am *not* scared of them!" I snapped, my voice rising. "But I'm worried that they might ride the horses too hard."

"That's not your problem," he said. "It's mine. I can handle these characters. When Matthew's not here, I'm in charge, remember? What I say goes, and

I say they ride. Now hurry up and bring out some horses!''

A skinny biker in a blue helmet snickered. ''Yeah, get with it. We don't have all day, right, Ace?''

''Right,'' said the beefy one, scowling at me. ''And we paid in advance, like the chick said. What's the matter, kid? Our cash not good enough for you?''

I gave up. Feeling very small and powerless, I stomped off into the stable, fuming every step of the way. I don't know if I was madder at the smart-aleck bikers or at Zach for ordering me around like that. Orville, silent as usual, helped me saddle the horses, then began leading them outside two by two.

Lydia came in just as I was taking Ariel out of her stall. ''I locked the cash box in the office,'' she told me. ''I didn't like the way those creeps were eyeballing the money. You're going with them, huh?''

''Better believe it,'' I said grimly. ''Mr. Hotshot I'm-in-Charge Wallace thinks he can control them by himself, but if they start acting up, he's going to need all the help he can get.''

''Then I'm coming, too,'' Lydia said, heading for Lucky's stall.

I'd had a bad feeling about those guys from the moment I set eyes on them, but I didn't expect things to be this awful. The trail ride was a nightmare from beginning to end. Zach gave his version of Matthew's safety lecture and we took off. The minute we left Matthew's property and started up the hill toward the woods, Ace let out a whoop.

"Ride 'em, cowboys!" he yelled, digging his heels into Baron's sides and swatting him on the rump. Startled, the black gelding broke into a canter that immediately turned into a clumsy gallop. In a flash he passed Zach and Moonshine, with the other bikers thundering behind, all clutching their saddles and hollering at the top of their lungs.

"Hey! Come back!" Zach shouted, taking off after them. "What do you think you're doing?"

"*Riding,* man!" a guy in a green helmet called over his shoulder. "These machines are built for speed!"

Ariel was dancing around, eager to join in the chase, but I held her back, unwilling to leave Lydia behind. "Are you all right?" I asked anxiously.

She nodded, patting Lucky's neck. "This has to be either the calmest horse in the world or the laziest—he couldn't care less about keeping up with the pack. Don't worry about us." As I gave the palomino her head, Lydia called after me, "Be careful, Tess!"

Ariel might have been small, but at a flat-out gallop, she was amazingly fast. Her hooves hardly seemed to touch the ground. I bent low over her neck like a jockey heading for the finish line, and we soon caught up with the last of the riders. It was the skinny biker, and he wasn't snickering anymore. He was hanging on to his saddle for dear life with both hands, and he looked terrified.

"How do you stop this thing?" he yelled. "If I fall off and break my neck, I'll sue!"

"If you fall off and break your neck, you'll be

dead," I yelled back, grabbing Lady's flapping reins. "And it'll be your own fault!"

Lady must have recognized my voice, because she slowed down at once. Even before she came to a complete stop, her rider slid to the ground. His knees buckled under him and he sat down hard, gasping for breath. Beneath that shiny blue helmet, his face was so pale, I was afraid he might pass out.

"You okay?" I asked, peering down at him from Ariel's back.

"Yeah—yeah, I guess so." He stood up gingerly. "Geez, was this ever a bum idea! Gimme bikes any day!"

I tossed Lady's reins to him. "Here. Get back on."

The guy stared at me. "You gotta be kidding! That horse is a killer!" he whined. "What is he—some kind of wild stallion or something?" Lady gazed at him mildly.

"*She* is a thirteen-year-old mare," I told him. "For your information, a mare is a female horse. Lady's one of the gentlest horses at The Barn. Now, are you going to get back on or not?"

"I'll think about it," he mumbled.

"If you need any help, my friend's on her way," I said. "Until then, you're on your own." Nudging Ariel gently with my heels, I urged her into a canter and soon caught up with the rest of the gang.

Between us, Zach and I managed to slow them down and herd them back to The Barn, but it wasn't easy, and it took a long time. All the horses were lathered, and Frenchie was limping. Matthew had returned by then. The minute we rode into the stable yard and my uncle saw the condition of our mounts, he was furious.

As we dismounted, my uncle said to Zach and me, "Take the horses inside. Have Orville check out Frenchie's leg and tell him I'll be right there." His gray eyes were steely, and his deep voice, usually so pleasant and mellow, sounded harsh.

Zach and I silently did as we were told, and Lydia helped us. As I led Ariel and Baron into the stable, I heard one of the bikers say, "Hey, you the boss of this outfit? We got a complaint. We paid for a whole hour, but we only rode for forty-five minutes."

"Yeah—we want our money back," another one demanded.

The three of us hurried outside as fast as we could. Though nobody said a word, I knew we were all thinking the same thing: If the Panthers were going to make more trouble, we didn't want Matthew facing them alone.

"There will be no refunds," Matthew said to the surly bikers, controlling himself with great effort. "You have mistreated my horses and lamed one of them. Get out, and don't come back. If you ever show your faces at The Barn again, I guarantee you'll regret it."

"Oh, yeah?" Ace sneered, swaggering up to him. "It's a free country, man. Nobody tells me where I can go or what I can do, get it?"

"That goes for the rest of us too," said the skinny biker, who was his nasty self again now that he'd recovered from his fright. The others nodded and mumbled in agreement.

Zach clenched his fists and took a step forward, but Matthew held him back. "I meant what I said. Leave *now*, before I forget that you're nothing but a bunch of kids and give you the whipping you deserve."

Ace laughed in his face. "You and who else, man?"

"Me, that's who!" Shaking off Matthew's restraining hand, Zach charged at the bully.

Lydia let out a shriek as the two boys swung viciously at each other, landing punches wherever they could.

By the time my uncle managed to separate them, Ace had a bloody nose, and Zach's left eye was beginning to swell up. As Ace stumbled out of the stable yard followed by his gang, he glared from Matthew to Zach.

"You'll be sorry—*real* sorry," he growled. "Nobody messes with the Panthers and gets away with it!"

"That's a risk I'm willing to take," Matthew said grimly.

The bikers revved their engines with an ear-splitting roar, then tore down the dirt road, leaving a cloud of exhaust fumes behind them. A moment later they were gone.

In the sudden silence I glanced apprehensively at my scowling uncle. I was sure he must be angry at Zach, and at me, too, and I didn't blame him. I blamed myself. Even though I had tried to talk Zach out of letting the bikers ride, I shouldn't have given up so fast.

"Matthew, I'm so sorry about . . ." I began, but Zach interrupted.

"You don't have anything to be sorry about," he said gruffly. Turning to Matthew, he added, "It was all my fault. Tess didn't want me to take them out, but I was too pigheaded to listen." He swallowed hard. "If you don't want me to work at The Barn anymore, I'll understand."

Matthew's expression softened. "Of course you're going to keep working here. You're my right-hand man," he said. "And I know I can trust you to use better judgment from now on."

Zach started to smile, then winced, touching his swollen face. I winced too in sympathy. His eye was turning purple, and I noticed that the knuckles of both his hands were grazed and bleeding.

"Better do something about those wounds of yours while I take a look at Frenchie's leg," Matthew added.

As Zach headed for the office where the first-aid kit was kept, Lydia said, "What if they come back?"

"I'm sure they won't," Matthew told her. "Blowhards like that are usually all talk and no action." Shaking his head, he said, "I'm sorry you had to be involved in this, Lydia. Nothing even remotely like it has ever happened before."

Lydia grinned, her green eyes sparkling behind her glasses. "Oh, I didn't mind, honestly. It was exciting! And Zach was so incredibly brave, beating up that bully the way he did. Maybe I'd better see how he's doing—I'm pretty good at first aid." With a wink at me, she headed toward the office.

As Matthew and I went into the stable, I suddenly remembered his trip to town. "Did you tell Mr. Brewster you weren't going to sell?" I asked eagerly.

Raising his eyebrows, Matthew said, "So you know all about that, do you?"

I nodded. "Edward told us. Mom and Dad and Sabrina think you're going to take the money and turn ordinary, but I was sure you wouldn't." Suddenly I had a terrible thought. What if I didn't know my uncle as well as I thought I did? What if he had said yes? "You didn't, did you? You're not going to let Mr. Brewster buy you out, are you?"

Matthew put his arm around me and gave me a quick hug. "No, Tess, I'm not going to sell The Barn. And don't worry—I'm not going to turn respectable, either!"

"Oh, good!" I let out a sigh of relief. "Then nothing's going to change. Everything will be just the way it's always been!"

We went into Frenchie's stall then, and Orville told Matthew in as few words as possible that the sorrel had apparently strained a tendon in his right foreleg.

Glad that it was nothing more serious, I left them to treat it while I took care of Ariel.

The palomino didn't seem any the worse for our adventure, thank goodness. After I took off her tack, rubbed her down, and made sure she had plenty of feed and fresh hay, I gave Ariel the last few pieces of apple and carrot, which I'd saved just for her.

"Well, that ride wasn't exactly peaceful, was it?" I asked, stroking her velvety nose. "But we'll make up for it tomorrow, I promise."

As I left Ariel's loose box, closing the door behind me, I wondered if Matthew had received Mr. Graham's check for her board. I'd have to ask him about that later. Meanwhile, I helped Zach and Lydia cool down and feed the other horses. Zach's left eye was swollen shut by now, his knuckles were bandaged, and a bruise was starting to appear on his jaw.

"What are you going to tell your mom?" I asked him as we piled hay into Moonshine's manger. "She'll freak out when she sees you."

Zach shrugged. "I'll tell her I got into a fight with six bozos who were giving Matthew a hard time."

"What do you mean, *six*?" I exclaimed. "You only fought with *one* of them!"

Grinning, he said, "Yeah, I know. But it makes a better story the other way." Then he added seriously, "I meant what I said to Matthew before, pipsqueak. I should have listened to you. And I'm sorry I yelled at you the way I did."

"You should be," I said with a sniff. "If you're

56

really sorry, how about not calling me 'pipsqueak' anymore? It drives me crazy!"

"Deal," Zach agreed, but there was a mischievous twinkle in his good eye. "Let's see—what'll I call you instead? How about small-fry? Or shrimp? Or . . ."

"Tess!" I hollered, throwing a fistful of hay at him. "Stop calling me names, you pigheaded turkey!"

"Look who's calling names now!" Zach shouted back. "So I'm a pigheaded turkey, am I? You asked for it, pipsqueak!" He snatched some hay out of Baron's manger and dumped it on my head.

"That does it! You're dead!" I sputtered. I grabbed a whole armload of hay and flung it at him.

"Help! I'm being attacked by a hay-throwing maniac!" he yelled. Laughing, he raced down the aisle between the stalls with me in hot pursuit, giggling and pelting him with handfuls of hay.

Lydia stepped out of Cinnamon's stall. "What on earth . . . ? Tess, what are you doing to poor Zach?" she cried.

Zach grabbed her around the middle, using her as a shield. "Save me from this madwoman! She's trying to turn me into a human haystack!"

"You're not human, you're a pigheaded turkey!" I shouted. "Out of the way, Lydia! Let me at him! He'll be sorry he ever called me a pipsqueak!"

"Watch out for his eye—*oof!*"

Lydia and Zach lost their balance as Zach swung her around, trying to keep her between himself and me, and I tripped over one of Zach's big feet. The three of us ended up in a tangle of arms, legs, and hay on the stable floor, scuffling and laughing like idiots while the horses peered at us curiously over their stall doors.

"Give up?" I panted at last, straddling Zach's chest and pinning his arms down on either side.

"Two battles in one day?"

I looked up to see Matthew smiling down at us. I loosened my grip on Zach's arms for just a second, but it was long enough for him to escape. He scrambled to his feet, leaving Lydia and me sprawled on the floor. Lydia's glasses had fallen off, and I helped her dig through the pile of hay until we found them.

"Sorry, Matthew," Zach said, running his fingers through his tousled hair. "We'll stop fooling around and get back to work. But this time it *wasn't* my fault, honest. I was minding my own business when pip—" I glared at him. "When *Tess* attacked me for no reason!"

"That's okay," Matthew said. "You kids had a pretty rough afternoon—you deserve some fooling-around time. Why don't you call it a day? Orville and I will take care of the rest of the horses and finish evening feed."

Though Zach insisted that he was perfectly capable of finishing his chores, he finally agreed to go home after we cleaned up the mess we'd made during our hay fight.

When we were finished, Lydia asked Zach

anxiously, "Will you be able to see well enough to drive?"

"No problem," Zach said. "That old heap of mine has made the trip so often that it could probably find its way home all by itself." He glanced at me, grinning. "You coming out again tomorrow? I need to know so I can be prepared—maybe I can find a suit of armor somewhere!"

"We sure are," Lydia said before I could open my mouth.

As Zach drove off in his ancient green clunker, Lydia gazed after him, a dreamy smile on her face. "I think he likes me," she sighed. "When we were tackling him, there was a wonderful moment when his beautiful hazel eyes met mine . . ."

"His *eye*, you mean," I corrected, giggling. "Was that before or after he knocked your glasses off?"

"He didn't knock them off," Lydia said indignantly. "At least, he didn't mean to. It was an accident. Oh, Tess, I think I'm in love!"

I groaned. "I can't *believe* this! You're doing it already!"

"What are you talking about? What am I doing?"

"Acting stupid and boring, just like Sabrina," I said, scowling at her.

Lydia giggled. "I am not! It's just that Zach's so different than I expected. He's so handsome, and so much fun, and so—so—"

"Pigheaded!" I finished. "Come on, Lydia. If you can come back down to earth, we'd better head for the bus stop. But first I want to talk to Matthew for a minute."

We found my uncle in the feed room. He was surprised to see us. "What are you two still doing here?" he asked.

"We're just leaving," I told him. "But—well, I'm worried about you. What if those bikers try something? They were pretty mad."

Matthew smiled. "Like I said before, I don't think they will. But if it'll set your mind at ease, I'll let Nemo and Flash run loose for the next few nights. They're pretty hopeless as guard dogs, but they make a lot of noise, and so do those motorcycles. If the gang comes back, I'll be sure to hear them, and I'll call the police."

"Promise?"

"Promise. Now you'd better hurry, girls, or you'll miss your bus."

There was one more thing I wanted to find out before we left. "Did Mr. Graham ever send a check for Ariel's board?"

"You know, I completely forgot about that," Matthew admitted, stroking his beard. "If he did, I haven't received it yet. But he only brought her here a few days ago. It'll probably come in next week's mail." He grinned at me. "Don't worry about that, too, Tess. I won't evict her because she's behind in her rent."

Lydia and I said good-bye, then started down the road to Route 22.

"What will happen if Ariel's owner doesn't pay up?" Lydia asked me.

I shrugged. "I guess Matthew would send Mr. Graham another bill."

"Yeah, that makes sense. But what if he doesn't *know* the address? Or what if Mr. Graham gave Matthew a *phony* address, because he's really a horse thief who stole this really valuable palomino!" Lydia's green eyes sparkled with excitement. "And the FBI is on his trail, so he had to dump her before he could make a clean getaway! Something like that happened in the mystery I just finished reading. I'll lend it to you, Tess—you'd love it! It's about a woman jockey who breaks up a ring of international horse thieves . . ."

Lydia kept on talking while we boarded the bus and took our seats, but I wasn't really listening. She'd just given me a wonderful, crazy idea. If Mr. Graham never came back, maybe Ariel could stay at The Barn forever!

~5~

Sunday wasn't as warm and beautiful as Saturday had been, but there were enough riders at The Barn to keep us busy every minute. The biker gang hadn't returned during the night. There was no sign of them that day, either, and I was so happy to be with Ariel that I soon forgot all about them.

The first full week of school was busy too. I tried out for the girls' volleyball team and made it, which meant practice a couple of days after school, and the teachers seemed to be making up for lost time over the summer by piling on tons of homework. Lydia and I walked to school together every morning and ate lunch with our group of friends, but aside from that and the classes we shared, we didn't see each other very much. That was okay, though, because we knew we'd be spending the next weekend together at The Barn. We were both counting the days until then, but for different reasons—Lydia couldn't wait to see Zach again, and I couldn't wait to see Ariel.

Everything was cool at home, too, until Thursday night. I'd gone straight to my room after volleyball practice to start my homework. I'd barely made a dent in it when I realized that it was time for dinner. I ran a comb through my hair and dashed downstairs to find my parents and Sabrina already seated at the dining-room table. None of them looked happy.

". . . So after Matthew turned down his first of-fer, Mr. Brewster made him another one this afternoon," Sabrina was saying as I sat down at my place. "He turned that one down too. Dad, he's *your* brother. Can't you talk some sense into him?"

Uh-oh, I thought. *Here it comes.* I'd been kind of surprised that nobody had said anything before about Matthew's refusal to sell. I certainly hadn't mentioned it, and I'd hoped that since the rest of the family hadn't either, they'd simply accepted his decision. Obviously I was wrong.

"Sabrina, I have been trying without success to talk sense into your uncle for longer than you've been alive. He's always been as stubborn as a mule," my father said grimly, serving himself some salad. "I ran into Brewster on the street today, and he told me all about it. Apparently the main reason Matthew

64

gave was that he feels a development at that location would be an ecological disaster."

"He's right, Dad," I said. "Building a bunch of houses on Matthew's property would upset the balance of nature. They'd probably cut down most of the trees. They might even drain the pond. Then the water birds wouldn't have any place to nest, and—"

"Oh, who cares about water birds!" Sabrina interrupted. "The point is, our uncle and Edward's father don't see eye to eye, and it's affecting my relationship with Edward. We were supposed to go out tomorrow night the way we always do, and today Edward canceled our date. If he breaks up with me, it'll be all Matthew's fault!"

I stared at my sister. "You mean Edward might ditch you because one of his father's business deals fell through? You've got to be kidding!" Then I grinned. "Look at it this way—you and Edward are star-crossed lovers, like Romeo and Juliet. Their families didn't see eye to eye either."

"That is *not* funny!" Sabrina snapped. "They also wound up *dead*!" Pushing back her chair, she stood up. "Mother, I'm not very hungry. May I please be excused?"

Before Mom could reply, Sabrina ran out of the room.

"Tess, you know you shouldn't tease your sister like that," my mother said, frowning. "She's very upset about this whole thing."

"But, Mom, it's none of her business! Matthew can

65

make his own decisions, and if Edward breaks up with her over this, then he's really not worth much, is he?"

"Tess is right," my father said. "This really doesn't concern Sabrina and Edward. It concerns me, however, as head of this family, and I'd really like Matthew to help me run the store."

"Can't you talk to him and make him see that selling his property is in his best interest?" my mother suggested.

"Why is it in Matthew's best interest to sell his land if he doesn't want to, Mom? He's not a businessman like Dad," I said. "He'd be miserable sitting behind a desk all day at the store, but he's perfectly happy where he is."

"That may be true, honey," my father said, "but I can't help worrying about Matthew. He's my younger brother, and I have to look out for him. I'd like to see him settled in a job that will give him security down the road. Can you understand that?"

I nodded. "Yes, I guess I can. It's not that you don't care about what Matthew wants. You just think you know better than he does what's good for him, and you don't think he can take care of himself."

"That's not what your father said," my mother insisted. "Don't you understand that we're concerned about your uncle? Now, Tess, tell us about your day. How did volleyball practice go?"

The subject of Matthew was officially closed, at least for the moment.

* * *

"So what happened when your father called Matthew yesterday?" Lydia asked Saturday morning on our way to The Barn.

"Not much. Nothing new, anyway," I said. "They talked for a long time, but I heard my dad telling my mom last night that Matthew wouldn't budge an inch. I didn't think he would and I'm glad he didn't, but I feel sorry for my dad. He's really worried about Matthew—I think he pictures him winding up homeless or something."

"Gee, that's too bad," Lydia murmured.

"There's more," I told her. "Dad got a call at his office yesterday afternoon from Eli Putnam. Old Man Putnam was really mad—he and his two sons had big plans for all the money Mr. Brewster was going to pay them for their farm, but Brewster won't buy it unless he can buy Matthew's, too. So after Old Man Putnam called Matthew and yelled at him, he called my father—he seems to think Dad can force Matthew to sell just because they're brothers. Then he started hollering and making all kinds of threats, so Dad hung up on him."

"Mr. Putnam sounds horrible," Lydia said.

"Well, he's definitely strange," I said. "Last summer a couple of cows wandered into one of his pastures from Mr. Wilcox's farm, and Old Man Putnam called the police—he wanted the cops to arrest the cows for trespassing! I've never actually met Mr. Putnam, but I've seen him a couple of times when I was riding past his place. He looks kind of like an old goat, and he shook his fist at me once and hollered something about me being a spy. I think he's some kind of a nut."

"What about his sons? Are they nuts too?" Lydia asked, fascinated.

I shrugged. "I wouldn't be surprised. I've never met them, either. Mr. Putnam and his older son, Charles, hardly ever leave the property, but Zach knows the younger one, Henry. They're both juniors at the Consolidated School, even though Henry's almost eighteen. Zach told me he was held back—he's not dumb, but he cuts a lot. Zach also said he's kind of strange—keeps to himself most of the time."

"Boy, some neighbors Matthew's got," Lydia said, shaking her head. Suddenly she grabbed my arm. "Tess! Look out the window!"

As the bus slowed to a stop opposite The Barn, I looked. What I saw made me gasp. The whole front of the stable was covered with graffiti in white spray paint, and right in the middle I could clearly read the words YOULL GET YOURS SHERILL in huge letters.

We got off the bus and raced down the dirt road to join Matthew, Orville, and Zach in the stable yard, where they were surveying the damage.

"Are the horses all right?" I cried, immediately thinking of Ariel. "They didn't hurt any of them, did they?"

"No, Tess, the horses are fine," Matthew assured me. "The graffiti 'artists' left their message and that

68

was all. It must have happened late last night, after I went to bed."

"I'll bet it was those bikers," Zach said, scowling. I noticed that his eye wasn't swollen anymore, but it was still pretty colorful. "Matthew doesn't think so, though."

"No, I don't," my uncle said. "I would have heard their motorcycles, and I didn't hear a thing, not even the dogs barking. It's possible that whoever it was brought meat or something to shut them up. Neither Nemo nor Flash ate much breakfast, which leads me to believe they might have had a hefty midnight snack."

"Maybe the meat was drugged," I suggested. "That's what the crooks did in the book Lydia loaned me. Are the dogs sluggish and dopey this morning?" Just then the two German shepherds came galloping into the stable yard, welcoming me in their usual frantic fashion. "No, I guess they weren't drugged. Fine watchdogs you are," I scolded, but they didn't look at all ashamed of themselves.

"Paint," Orville mumbled.

"Right, Orville," Matthew said. "Let's cover up this mess before any riders show up. There's some paint in the shed out back. With all five of us working, it shouldn't take long."

Half an hour later the ugly words had disappeared beneath a fresh coat of red paint. "I still say Ace and his gang did it," Zach insisted, tossing the empty paint cans into the garbage bin. "They probably left their bikes somewhere and sneaked up on foot. That would explain why you didn't hear anything, Matthew. And they *did* threaten you, remember."

"Wait a minute!" Lydia exclaimed. "Those bikers aren't the only ones who have a grudge against Matthew. Tess was just telling me that Mr. Putnam's really mad at him."

"That's right," I said to my uncle. "Maybe his sons graffitied the stable to scare you into selling out!"

"It's possible, I suppose," he said wearily. "But in the first place, there's no evidence pointing to them, the bikers, or anyone else, for that matter. In the second place, petty vandalism isn't all that uncommon, unfortunately, not even out here in the country. It could have been the work of some bored kids from town with nothing better to do on a Friday night, or even part of a fraternity hazing at the college." He turned to Orville. "I guess we'd better keep watch for the next couple of nights, in case whoever it was tries something else. I'll do it tonight, and you can take over tomorrow night. I'll pay you overtime, of course. That okay with you?"

"Yep," Orville said. His pale-blue eyes brightened. "Shotgun?"

"Absolutely not!" Matthew said. "No violence. There's too much of that in the world as it is. If anybody shows up, we'll call the sheriff and let him handle it." Orville looked disappointed. "Now I suggest we get on with our chores."

As he and Orville went into the stable, I said, "There must be *some* evidence. We just haven't looked for it, that's all."

Lydia nodded enthusiastically. "Yeah—every criminal slips up sooner or later. There's no such thing as a perfect crime. I bet if we search very carefully, we'll find at least one clue."

"Footprints!" I exclaimed. "The yard's still pretty muddy from yesterday's rain. Whoever it was had to leave footprints!"

"So did we," Zach pointed out. "We've been walking all over the place. How are you going to tell the difference between our footprints and someone else's?"

"I hadn't thought about that," I admitted.

"It still wouldn't hurt to look around," Lydia said. "Who knows? We might find something the vandals dropped—like a wallet with ID!"

"Yeah, right. And maybe a signed confession," Zach scoffed. "You two are nuts, you know that?"

He helped us poke around for a while in the mud anyway, but we didn't come up with anything except one rusty old horseshoe and a broken pink barrette. Then a car full of riders drove up, putting an end to our search.

I hadn't given up, though, not by a long shot. I was positive there had to be a clue somewhere, and I was determined to find it. We might have painted out the words on the stable, but I could still see them in my mind: YOULL GET YOURS SHERILL. To me, it meant that the vandals hadn't given up either. If we didn't track them down, they'd be back, and the next time, they might do something a whole lot worse.

I couldn't forget about my worries that day, not even when I was riding Ariel. Each time I took her out, the palomino mare amazed me all over again. She had such a smooth trot I didn't even have to post. Her mouth was so tender that when I wanted her to slow down, all I had to do was apply the slightest pressure on the reins, and a gentle nudge of my heels made her quicken her pace. She was a dream horse, all right. The only thing I could think of that would be worse than having her owners take her away would be if somebody harmed her. That's what I was afraid the vandals might do if they came back, so between trail rides I kept scouting around for clues every chance I got.

Lydia helped me look, and late in the afternoon she found something in the tall grass around the corner of the stable—an empty spray can. We were both really excited.

"Look, Zach!" Lydia cried triumphantly, showing it to him. "Evidence!"

Zach wasn't impressed. "Big deal. The only thing it tells us that we didn't know before is the brand of paint the guys used. What good will that do?"

"Plenty," I said. "We can take this can to all the hardware stores in town and ask if anybody bought several of them recently. The vandals had to buy more than one—maybe five or six! Whoever sold that many cans would be sure to remember."

"Yes, and I bet there are fingerprints on this one!" Lydia added.

"There sure are," Zach agreed. "Lots of 'em, including yours."

Lydia looked dismayed. "Oh, wow! I never even thought about that. Some detective I am."

"Don't worry about the fingerprints, Lydia," I said. "It's the can itself that's important. We'll start checking out the hardware stores on Monday. I'm going to look around a little more, just in case there's something we missed."

I didn't really think I'd find anything, and I was about to call it a day when something shiny under the bench by the office door caught my eye. When I picked it up, I saw that it was a small, round metal object. I recognized it right away—a silver stud, the kind I'd noticed on the Panthers' leather jackets!

"This proves it! It had to be the motorcycle gang!" I said to Lydia. "Once we get a description from the hardware store where they bought the paint, all we have to do is track them down and confront them with the evidence. And if they don't confess, then we tell the sheriff. It'll be an open-and-shut case!"

Zach had been pretending not to listen, but now he said, "I don't know if it proves anything or not— that stud could have fallen off when I was beating up that Ace turkey. But like I was telling Matthew

73

before, I think the bikers did it. You'd better not go after them by yourselves, though. They might get nasty. If you find out anything, let me know, okay?"

"Okay!" Lydia and I said together.

As we finished cleaning the saddles and bridles and putting them away in the tack room, Lydia whispered to me, "This is so thrilling! And it'll be so romantic if Zach has to rescue us."

"Lydia, give me a break. We're not going to need rescuing. Just because we're female doesn't mean we're fragile." I frowned. "I wish the hardware stores in town were open on Sunday. The sooner we can find out who bought the paint, the sooner we'll be able to nail them."

"Yes, but in the meantime they won't be able to pull anything with Matthew, Orville, and the dogs standing guard," Lydia said.

"You never can tell. Matthew and Orville won't be doing it together, and one person can't be everywhere at once. Somebody could sneak across the back pasture in the dark and enter the barn without being seen from the front and do a lot of damage." I shivered at the thought. "We just have to hope we can find them before they figure that out!"

~6~

That evening the weather changed. It started to rain while Lydia and I were waiting for the bus, and soon it was pouring buckets. Poor Fred could hardly see to drive, and it took us almost an hour to reach our stop. By the time we got off, the temperature must have dropped by about twenty degrees, and a fierce wind was whipping golden leaves off the maple trees along Brookfield Street. There was no question about it—it wasn't summer anymore.

When I staggered up the walk to my house, I was soaked to the skin and my teeth were chattering. My father flung open the front door and my mother hustled me upstairs without even waiting for me to take off my boots. They had been watching out the window, waiting for me, worried sick when I was so late getting home. Dad told me that according to the weather report on TV, a major storm was sweeping up the coast, and Stockton was being lashed by the tail of it.

While my mother helped me peel off my wet clothes, Sabrina ran a hot tub, overflowing with her own special, scented bubble bath. With all the attention I was getting, I didn't think to mention what had happened at The Barn. Or maybe I forgot accidentally-on-purpose because I was afraid my parents wouldn't let me go out there anymore if they knew. It would be awful to be separated from Ariel.

Besides, Lydia and I were dying to go on Matthew's Harvest Moon Trail Ride. It was always scheduled for the Saturday nearest to the September full moon. I'd never been allowed to go before, because my parents thought I was too young to ride at night, even under my uncle's supervision. But this year they had decided that almost fifteen was old enough. It was going to be great.

As it turned out, the storm kept up all night and the following day, so we didn't go to The Barn on Sunday. I didn't really mind, and I figured that the horses had to be safe because the vandals wouldn't want to get cold and wet either.

The rain began to taper off on Monday. On Tuesday the skies were clear again, and the air was cool and autumn crisp. After school Lydia and I started checking out the paint and hardware stores in Stockton. There weren't many of them, and by Tuesday evening, we'd hit them all, with no results. Only two stores carried the particular brand of spray paint we asked about, and none of the clerks remembered selling a lot of cans of any brand at all.

Though our spray-can clue hadn't led anywhere, that didn't discourage us—not at first, anyway. Over the next few days we went to all the service stations in town, thinking that the Panthers might have needed gas or something for their bikes, but apparently they hadn't. Then we decided that maybe they'd stopped somewhere for a bite to eat, so we checked out Basta Pizza, Scanlon's Luncheonette, and even Mary's Tea Shoppe, where the little old ladies go, but nobody recalled seeing six boys who matched our descriptions of them. It seemed as though the biker gang had dropped off the face of the earth—or at least off the face of Stockton, Connecticut.

"Not even Sherlock Holmes could crack this case," Lydia said with a sigh, and I thought she was probably right.

In fact, I was beginning to wonder if there was a case to crack. When Lydia and I went to The Barn that Saturday, Matthew told us that Frenchie's leg was healing nicely and there had been no more incidents. I was glad to see that except for blowing down one of the old trees by the pond, the storm hadn't done much damage either.

There weren't many renters now that the weather had turned colder, so though we went on a couple of trail rides, Lydia, Zach, and I spent most of our time on Saturday and Sunday cleaning the stalls, grooming the horses, and saddle-soaping tack. On Sunday my uncle suggested that Zach and I exercise some of the boarders' horses. Naturally, I rode Ariel, while Zach rode a rangy roan named Moose whose owner was out of town on business and Lydia came along on good old reliable Lucky. She had been giving Lucky lots of special attention since she had started riding him, and it made me feel less guilty about spending so much time with Ariel.

As we ambled down our favorite trail through the woods, Zach said, "You guys coming on the Harvest Moon Trail Ride next Saturday?"

"We wouldn't miss it for the world," Lydia burbled. "It sounds *so* romantic!"

"I don't know about romantic," Zach said, "but it's fun. A lot of people have signed up already, including most of the boarders. It starts at eight o'clock and if the sky's clear, we ride all the way to the river and back under the harvest moon."

I leaned down and patted the palomino's silky shoulder. "I hope it's not cloudy—Ariel will look wonderful by moonlight."

The three of us rode along in silence for a few minutes. Finally Zach said, "Mr. Graham still hasn't paid for Ariel's board, Tess. Matthew sent him a bill last week to his New Jersey address." He glanced at me. "Tomorrow she'll have been here three weeks. Mr. Graham told Matthew she wouldn't be staying longer than that. Maybe he plans on paying when he picks her up." After a brief pause, he went on, "What I'm trying to say is—well, Ariel might be gone by Saturday."

"Oh, Tess, I forgot all about that!" Lydia said softly.

"Me too," I mumbled. The sudden lump in my throat felt as big as a volleyball. "Or at least, I tried to." I swallowed hard. "Zach, if he comes to take her away, will you—will you call me? Please?"

Zach nodded. None of us spoke much after that. The beauty of the autumn afternoon had been spoiled, and it wasn't long before we headed back to The Barn.

On Monday I went from class to class like a zombie, unable to concentrate on anything except Ariel. Was Mr. Graham leading her into the trailer while I struggled through a geometry quiz? When I was stumbling through a translation in French class, was Ariel on the Merritt Parkway? I couldn't even smile when I got an A+ from my English teacher on my essay because I was picturing Ariel's trailer speeding down the New Jersey Turnpike.

I didn't have volleyball practice after school, but Lydia had to attend a special meeting of the newspaper staff, so I walked home alone. When I checked our answering machine, the red light wasn't flashing, which meant there were no messages. Did that mean Mr. Graham hadn't taken Ariel away yet, or had Zach just forgotten to phone? *That would be just like him*, I thought gloomily. I was just about to call Matthew's number to find out if anything had happened when the phone rang. I picked up the receiver.

"Hello. Sherrill residence."

"Hi, Tess," said a familiar voice. "It's Zach. I figured you'd be getting home around now. Guess what?"

I sank into the chair next to the phone table, suddenly weak in the knees. "What?" I whispered.

"The bill came back!"

"Huh?"

"The bill—the one Matthew mailed to Mr. Graham! It came back marked 'Addressee Unknown—Return to Sender.' Then Matthew tried to get his phone number from information, but it's unlisted. What a crock! It's like I said when he left Ariel at The Barn—the guy's a deadbeat! He's dropped out of sight, so I guess that means the palomino's not going anywhere, at least not for a while."

"Omigosh!" If I hadn't already been sitting down, I probably would have collapsed on the floor. "You're kidding! You're *not* kidding, are you? Tell me you're not kidding!" I babbled. "Oh, Zach, that's terrific! It's the best news in the world!" Though I knew that Mr. Graham's disappearance didn't mean he'd never come back for Ariel, I couldn't help hoping for some kind of miracle.

"I kinda thought you'd be interested," he said, and I could just picture the broad grin on his face.

"Oh, by the way, Matthew says not to worry. It's okay by him if the palomino stays. So I'll see you on Saturday for the Harvest Moon Trail Ride, right?"

"Of course!" I cried. "I can't wait to tell Lydia. And, Zach, thanks for calling. I was afraid maybe you'd forget."

"How could I forget?" Zach sounded oddly gentle. "I know how much that mare means to you. You kind of light up every time you look at her." Then he added in his normal tone, "Well, gotta go, Tess. See you."

He's not nearly as obnoxious as he used to be, I thought as I hung up the phone. *In fact, he's really a pretty nice guy. And cute, too.* I shook my head to clear it. What was the matter with me? I was getting to be as bad as Lydia.

When I finally reached Lydia that evening, I had even more good news. After I told her about Ariel, I said, "And listen to this! At supper tonight I found out that my parents are taking Sabrina to look at colleges this weekend. They're leaving Saturday morning, and they won't be back until Sunday night. Believe it or not, I actually talked them into letting me stay with Matthew while they're gone! I just called him, and he said it would be fine. He invited you, too. Can you come?"

"I hope so," she said. "Hang on—I'll ask Mom and Dad right now." She came back on the line in about two seconds to say that her parents had given their permission. Then she launched into a long description of that afternoon's meeting of the *Advocate* staff. ". . . And when it was over, Jeremy treated me to a soda at Scanlon's," she finished.

"Who's Jeremy?"

Lydia heaved an exasperated sigh. "Haven't you been listening? He's the new Special Features editor, and he's really cute—almost as cute as Zach, but not quite."

"That's nice," I said vaguely. I was still on cloud nine, knowing that Ariel was waiting for me at The Barn. "You can tell me all about him tomorrow on the way to school."

Lydia giggled. "Boy, you really *are* out of it! I *have* been telling you all about him, you nitwit! But I'll tell you again tomorrow anyway. Maybe I'll tell Zach, too, when I see him. If he thinks I'm interested in somebody else, he might get a little jealous. And who knows what that could lead to under the harvest moon?"

My parents and Sabrina got an early start on Saturday morning. Sabrina wasn't very enthusiastic. She wanted to go to Whitfield next year because that's where Edward was, but my parents wanted her to look at a few other colleges before she made up her mind.

Shortly after they left, I met Lydia at the bus stop, and by half past nine we were stowing our gear in the bedroom Matthew had prepared for us. Like everything else in my uncle's big old house, it was simple and spare, and it had a kind of musty smell because he didn't have overnight guests very often. But the sunlight streaming through the red-gold leaves of the tree outside the window and the bright crazy quilts on the two mismatched beds made it warm and cozy. We didn't stay there long, though. There was work to be done in the stable, and I was itching to give Ariel the treats I'd brought—golden Delicious apples, her favorite kind.

As always the morning passed quickly. Around noon Zach and Matthew drove off to the feed store in my uncle's pickup truck, leaving Orville in charge. Things were pretty quiet, so Lydia and I decided to eat our lunch. We were just finishing our sandwiches when a little dark-green sports car pulled into the parking area next to the stable yard. To my amazement, Edward Brewster got out, looking like an ad for what the well-dressed hunter should wear, in a neon-orange vest and matching cap.

"What's he doing here?" I murmured to Lydia. "Edward's never come to The Barn before in his entire life!"

Edward strolled over to where we were sitting on the bench by the office door. "Hi," he said with an engaging grin. "If you're wondering why I'm wearing this getup, Dad and I went deer hunting this morning." He must have seen me cringe, because he added hastily, "But we didn't shoot anything, Tess, honest. Anyway, with Sabrina gone, I was feeling kind of lonely, so I thought I'd stop and take a look at this place. I figure it has to be pretty special since your uncle refuses to sell, even though Dad just upped his offer for the second time."

"It *is* special," I said. "Matthew's not here right now, but Lydia and I can show you around, if you like." I felt the least I could do was be polite. Otherwise I was sure to hear about it later from Sabrina.

Edward was interested, so we took him around the property, from the paddocks, the pond, and the exercise ring all the way to the woods. We came back by way of the orchard and Matthew's vegetable garden, and finished by taking him through the stable and introducing him to some of the horses, saving Ariel for last. I gave Edward a capsule version of her story, and when he saw her, he let out a long, low whistle.

"What a beauty!" he said admiringly. "No wonder you're so crazy about her, Tess. I don't know anything about horses, but this one looks like a Thoroughbred."

Ariel tossed her pretty little head and snorted as if she appreciated the compliments, and we all laughed. Then I gave Edward an apple slice, showing him how to offer it to her on the palm of his hand. He was a little nervous, but I assured him she wouldn't bite, and of course she didn't.

As we walked out into the sunlight, I found myself actually warming up to Edward for the first time. "Tonight's the Harvest Moon Trail Ride," I told him impulsively. "It's going to be a lot of fun. Do you want to come?"

"Yes, why don't you," Lydia added. "You don't have to be a great rider—there'll be plenty of supervision."

Edward laughed. "I'm not any kind of rider at all. I've never been on a horse in my life, unless you count the horses on the merry-go-round, and I even managed to fall off one of those when I was about six years old! I think I'd better pass. Besides, I have a major exam coming up on Monday, and without Sabrina to distract me, I'm going to spend the rest of the weekend cramming. Thanks for inviting me, though."

Lydia and I walked him to his car. Right before he got in, he paused. "You know, I just thought of something. Some of my friends at Whitfield might be interested in that trail ride. What time does it start?"

"Eight o'clock," I told him, "and it should end around nine thirty. But if anybody wants to go, they ought to call and make a reservation, or there may not be enough horses to go around."

"Okay, I'll mention it. Thanks for the tour," Edward said, starting the engine. "And, Tess, please tell your uncle I'm sorry I missed him."

As he drove away, Lydia said, "What a nice guy! Sabrina's lucky to have a boyfriend like Edward. Why don't you like him, Tess?"

"I never said I didn't like him," I protested. "I just thought he was kind of boring, that's all. Maybe that's because I never spent much time with him before. I guess Sabrina *is* pretty lucky after all."

Unfortunately Edward wasn't the only visitor to The Barn that afternoon, and the others weren't nearly so pleasant. A few riders had just left, and Zach, Lydia, and I were unsaddling their horses when we heard a commotion outside—barking and loud, angry shouting.

"Maybe it's the bikers!" Lydia gasped.

"Good!" Zach said, striding out of Calico's stall. "This time I'm going to beat those jerks to a pulp, all six of them!"

I ran after him, calling, "Zach, wait . . ."

But when we ran into the stable yard, we didn't see six Panthers. Instead we saw three Putnams—Eli and his two sons, Charles and Henry. Old Man Putnam was doing all the yelling. Matthew was holding back the dogs while Orville, who had been helping my uncle replace some rotted boards in the upper level of the stable, glowered down from the top of his ladder.

"You got no right!" Mr. Putnam was shouting, his goatish beard jutting only inches from Matthew's face. "That Brewster fella was gonna buy my farm until you said you wouldn't sell. You done me and my boys outa our rightful profit, and that ain't neighborly. That ain't right!"

"Right," said Charles, glaring sullenly at Matthew. He must have been about twenty, tall and wiry, with beady little eyes like his father. I thought he looked like a weasel.

"Right," Henry, the younger brother, echoed. His thin, pinched face was even weaselier than Charles's, and his bony shoulders were hunched beneath an obviously new black-leather jacket very much like the ones the bikers had been wearing.

"Who are those guys? The Right Brothers?" Lydia whispered with a nervous giggle.

"That's Old Man Putnam and his sons," I whispered back.

Her eyes widened. "Oh—the nut family. Bad news."

"Me and the boys was gonna move to California," Mr. Putnam ranted on. "We was maybe gonna buy an avocado ranch and make a decent living for a change. No way a man can make ends meet farming that land of mine. Only thing we got plenty of is rocks!"

Charles nodded, scowling, and Henry muttered, "Yeah. We can't afford to turn down all that money like you can, you and your fancy horses. We're not filthy rich like the Sherrills."

"Matthew isn't rich," Zach said angrily. "He's just trying to make a living the same as you. And he works a heck of a lot harder!"

Henry frowned at him. "What do you know about how hard we work, Wallace? You don't know nothing about nothing!"

"Oh yeah?"

Zach took a step toward Henry, but Matthew shot him a warning glance. "That's enough, Zach." Turning to Mr. Putnam, he said, "I understand that you're upset, Eli, and I'm sorry. But we've been over all this before. I'm not going to change my mind."

"If he don't sell, how am I supposed to pay for this here jacket and that motorbike I ordered?" Henry whined to his father. "You said we were gonna be rich."

Mr. Putnam scowled at him. "Shut your face, Henry. Let me do the talking." To Matthew he said, "I'm not just upset, Sherrill. I'm mad—real mad! You ain't gonna do me and my boys outa what's rightfully ours. We'll be leaving now, but you ain't seen the last of us, no sir! I'm gonna get me a lawyer, and then we'll see what's what. Don't say I didn't warn you!"

Nemo growled, and Flash let out a short, sharp bark. Only Matthew's tight grip on their collars prevented them from springing at the Putnams as they slouched out of the stable yard and climbed into their rattletrap pickup. After a few false starts, a couple of coughs, and a wheeze, the truck lurched down the road to Route 22.

"No good," said Orville, shaking his head. "Mean and lazy, all three of 'em."

"That's about the size of it, I'm afraid." Matthew released the dogs, who trotted off in the direction of the house. "But I pity those kids. If their mother hadn't died when they were little, the boys might have turned out differently. From what I hear, she was a nice lady. Raised by a father like that, they never had a chance."

"Old Man Putnam sure has a lot of nerve," I said indignantly. "What did he mean about getting a lawyer? To hear him talk, you'd think Mr. Brewster had already paid him the money and you stole it!"

"Yeah, and Henry's already spending it," Zach said. "Did you get a load of that jacket? Next thing you know, he'll be joining the Panthers."

"If he can find them," Lydia put in.

"To answer your question, Tess, there's no lawyer in the world who would take Eli's case, because he has no case," Matthew said. "Whenever he gets mad —and he's always mad at somebody for something —Eli threatens to sue. It's become a standing joke around here. Nobody takes him seriously, and neither do I." He picked up a length of board and began climbing up the ladder next to Orville's.

As Lydia and I went back into the barn, she said, "You know, it's too bad your uncle never got married and had children. I bet he'd be a wonderful father."

"I bet he would too," I agreed. "But it's probably too late now. Matthew's pretty old—he's almost thirty-six. Besides, how would he ever meet anybody? He spends all his time out here, and you just saw what his neighbors are like."

We had just finished unsaddling the horses when Zach came in. "Three more people just signed up," he told us. "Don't take any more reservations—we just ran out of horses. There'll be twenty-five riders tonight. This is going to be the biggest, best Harvest Moon Trail Ride ever!"

~7~

All day long I kept looking up at the sky, hoping it would stay bright and clear, and it did. When the sun finally sank behind the western mountains, only a few ribbons of purple cloud streaked the rosy-orange glow.

"It's so beautiful," Lydia said with a sigh, pausing to look out Matthew's kitchen window after we set the table for supper. "You don't see sunsets like that in town."

"No, you don't," Matthew said. "That's one of the reasons I don't live there." He turned off the flame under the pot he'd been stirring on his big, old-fashioned stove. "Well, looks like supper's ready."

I brought over three blue-and-white pottery bowls, and Matthew filled them with thick, deli-cious-smelling vegetable chowder. It was a simple meal—the soup, a crusty loaf of whole-grain bread, and the salad Lydia and I had made—but nothing had ever tasted so good to me.

"How did you learn to cook, Matthew?" I asked. "Daddy's great at barbecuing, but he's hopeless in the kitchen."

Smiling, my uncle said, "When you live alone, you learn to cook or you don't eat."

Lydia sliced off a thick slab of bread (her third) and slathered it with butter. "Cooking's not all that hard, but baking is something else. This is the best bread I've ever tasted, and I bet it didn't come from a store."

"You're right, but I'm afraid I can't take credit for that," Matthew said. "A friend gave it to me. She does all her own baking, and she keeps me well supplied. We'll be having some of her oatmeal-raisin cookies for dessert."

I swear I could see Lydia's ears prick up just the way Ariel's did when I offered the palomino a treat. I knew she was remembering our conversation about my uncle that afternoon. She was probably adding up female friend, bread, and cookies and coming up with romance, which was pretty silly. Then I thought about the bread Sabrina had baked to impress Edward a few weeks ago. Could Lydia possibly be right? Was there a woman in Matthew's life that nobody knew anything about?

No way, I decided. The baked goods were probably a gift from old Mrs. Trumbull. She and her husband owned the farm where my uncle bought his butter and eggs. Mrs. Trumbull sold homemade bread and jellies, too, and I knew she liked Matthew a lot. Yes, that had to be it.

When we had finished our supper, washed the dishes, and fed the dogs, it was almost seven thirty. It had gotten really chilly after the sun went down, so we bundled up in windbreakers, scarves, and gloves, and headed for the stable. As we walked briskly along, with Flash and Nemo running in circles around us, a huge orange moon was just beginning to rise.

"That's a real harvest moon, all right," Matthew said. "She doesn't always cooperate on the night of the ride, but tonight it looks like we're in luck."

When we got to the barn, Zach and Orville were already saddling the horses. My uncle, Lydia, and I helped, and soon the riders began to arrive. There were people of all ages, from teenagers to grandparent types, and everybody was in high spirits, as excited as I was to be going out on this beautiful, crystal-clear night.

After all the renters and boarders were mounted, Matthew rode Othello, his coal-black gelding, out into the stable yard, followed by Zach on Moonshine. I gave Ariel some of the cookies I'd saved, led her out of her stall, and sprang into the saddle. Ariel was as excited about the ride as I was. I could feel the tension in her muscles beneath my legs. She shifted her weight anxiously, eager to be out under the bright moon on such a crisp autumn night. I whispered some soothing words into her alert ears, but I knew she wouldn't be satisfied until we were on the trail. We left the barn, and Lydia was waiting for me on Lucky, who seemed to be taking the whole adventure much more in stride. We rode out together to join the other riders. By then the moon had cleared the mountaintops. It was so enormous that it seemed to fill the entire sky, like a gigantic, glowing pumpkin.

Now that everyone was assembled, Matthew and Zach lined everybody up in pairs, placing Lydia and me somewhere in the middle, with instructions to keep an eye on the riders in front of us in case anyone needed help. I think Lydia was a little disappointed not to be paired up with Zach, but if she was, she didn't mention it.

Then Matthew delivered his safety lecture, adding, "Most of you have ridden here before, so you've heard all this many times. But riding at night, even by the light of this magnificent harvest moon, is very different from riding during the day. Your horses may get spooked by strange sounds or shadows, so have fun, but please be on the alert." He trotted to the front of the group. "Everybody ready?" he called out. Everybody was. "Any questions?" No questions. "Okay, then. Let's go!"

We set out with Matthew in the lead and Zach bringing up the rear. Orville, who as far as I knew had never been on a horse in his life, stayed behind with the dogs to keep watch while we were gone.

Matthew was right—the familiar landscape looked strange and magical by moonlight. It might even have seemed a little eerie if it hadn't been for the laughter and happy voices of the riders. As Matthew led the group along the road up the hill to the woods, somebody started singing "Shine On, Harvest Moon," and soon the rest of us joined in. After that we sang, "By the Light of the Silvery Moon," "In the Evening by the Moonlight," and every other "moon" song anybody could think of. The older people knew all the words, but Lydia and I just hummed along.

"I'm having a great time," Lydia said to me between songs.

"Even though you're stuck with me instead of Zach?" I teased.

"Well, you're not exactly the romantic partner I had in mind," Lydia admitted with a grin, "but you're still my best friend, so I guess I could do a lot worse."

We were entering the woods now, where the road narrowed to a trail barely wide enough to ride two abreast. I must have ridden this very same trail dozens of times, but never at night. During the day the leafy branches overhead formed a thick canopy that made it cool and pleasant no matter how hot the weather was. At night those same branches shut out most of the moonlight, and fallen leaves carpeted the trail so the horses' hooves made only a faint rustling sound. The riders' voices were suddenly hushed too. It was so dark that I could hardly see the horses in front of me, and so quiet that the mournful hoot of an owl made a shiver run down my spine. It startled Ariel, too. She tossed her head and snorted nervously.

"It's all right, girl," I murmured, stroking her shoulder. "It was just an owl—nothing to worry about."

"Brrr!" Lydia said softly. "Spooky, isn't it? Makes you realize that Halloween's only a month away."

Looking up ahead now, I could see moonlight filtering through the leaves. Matthew and the first few riders had almost reached the other side of the woods. In just a few minutes we would all be out in the open, picking up the road that led to the river. I knew it was silly, but I was relieved to be leaving that long, dark tunnel behind. It *was* spooky, and much too quiet.

And then suddenly it wasn't quiet anymore.

A volley of gunshots rang out, shattering the silence. People screamed, horses whinnied in terror, and the orderly procession exploded into a wild stampede. I've never been so scared in my entire life! Horses bolted in all directions—across the moonlit fields, down the river road, back into the woods. Ariel reared—something I had never seen her do before—and it was all I could do to calm her down. Even placid old Lucky broke into a canter. When I saw that Lydia seemed to be handling him all right, Ariel and I raced off to help Matthew and Zach round up the other horses and their frightened riders. For a moment I thought I heard another sound mingled with the beat of the palomino's pounding hooves, kind of like the roar of a distant engine—maybe a motorcycle, or a low-flying plane—but it didn't really register at the time. The only thing on my mind was how awful it would be if anyone got hurt.

Many of the riders were experienced enough to bring their mounts under control by themselves, but others were in real trouble. I did the best I could to help, and so did Lydia and some of the better riders, but it was Matthew and Zach who were the real heroes that night. They seemed to be everywhere at once, capturing runaway horses, reassuring frightened riders, and checking out the ones who had been thrown for injuries. Fortunately there weren't many of those, and the fallen riders remounted right away.

It seemed to take forever to gather all the horses and riders together again, though I guess it wasn't more than half an hour. By some miracle nobody appeared to have suffered more than a few bruises and a bad scare. But nobody felt like going on, and not even the best riders objected when Matthew announced that we would be returning immediately to The Barn. My first Harvest Moon Trail Ride had ended in a way I never could have imagined in a million years!

Instead of retracing our path through the woods on our way back, we followed a road that skirted the trees. This time there was no laughter, no happy chatter, and no singing. The riders who weren't still too shaken to speak kept asking each other the same questions: Who could have fired the shots, and why?

True, it was deer-hunting season, but deer hunters never went out after dark. It was possible, though, that somebody had been hunting raccoons. There had been reports of rabid coons in the area, and a bounty was being offered for each dead animal that was brought to Stockton's town hall. I heard one man say that coon hunting at night was a popular pastime among the local farmers.

Lydia and I were the last riders in the group, and after a while Zach rode back to join us. "You guys okay?" he asked.

"We're fine," I said, and Lydia nodded. "Just a little shook up, that's all. How about you?"

"I'm okay," Zach said. In the moonlight his scowling face looked almost as pale as the gray gelding's coat. "But I'm real mad at the idiot who fired those shots—he had to know there were a lot of people and horses coming down the trail. I wanted to try and find him, but Matthew wouldn't let me. He said it might be dangerous."

"He was absolutely right," Lydia exclaimed. "What if the person was still there? You could have been killed!" She glanced over at the dark mass of trees off to our right and shuddered. "I'd feel a lot better if we were in the middle of the group instead of at the end," she said nervously.

"No problem," Zach said. "We can go join the others. Coming, Tess?"

I shook my head. "You go ahead. Ariel and I will catch up with you in a few minutes." I decided the least I could do was let Lydia ride in the moonlight with Zach, even if it was just for a few minutes. Maybe then the ride wouldn't seem like such a big disappointment.

As for me, I wasn't frightened anymore. We'd had a terrifying experience, but it was over now. The only thing to do was try to forget the whole night. Gazing out over the moonlit fields from Ariel's back, I could hardly believe it had actually happened. The night was so peaceful, so still . . .

I don't know what made me glance over at the woods. Maybe I caught a glimpse of movement out of the corner of my eye. Whatever the reason, I turned my head and saw a figure on horseback emerging from the shadows into the moonlight. It wasn't one of our group, that was for sure—all Matthew's riders had been accounted for. Suddenly my heart was pounding so hard that I could hardly breathe. If only I'd gone with Lydia and Zach instead of staying behind!

Ariel was startled, too. She shied, and I tightened

my grip on the reins, whispering, "Easy, girl. It's okay." But I didn't think it was.

"Need any help?" the rider called out, coming closer. "Is everyone all right?" I was so surprised to hear a woman's voice that all I could do was stare.

She rode up next to me, but I couldn't really see what she looked like because her riding helmet shadowed her face. I couldn't even tell if she was young or old. "I heard the shots," she went on. "I knew about the trail ride, and I was afraid someone might have been hurt."

"Who—who are you?" I stammered, wishing with all my heart that the other riders weren't so far away. "What are you doing here?"

"I'm Joanna Talley. I often ride at night. I own Greenbriar Stables—ever heard of it?"

I nodded. I'd heard of it, all right, and Joanna Talley, too. According to my parents, she had a major grudge against our whole family, particularly Matthew.

"And who are *you*?" the woman asked.

Raising my chin and hoping I sounded braver than I felt, I said, "Theresa Sherrill. Matthew Sherrill's my uncle."

After a brief pause, she said, "I see. They call you Tess, don't they?"

"My *friends* call me Tess," I said sharply. "Excuse me, please. I have to catch up with the rest of the group." I dug my heels into Ariel's sides with more force than usual, and the palomino sprang forward.

As we cantered down the road, I heard the woman calling after us, "Tell your uncle to be careful, Theresa Sherrill. He may not know it, but he's made some enemies!"

Her words kept ringing in my ears while Ariel and I sped past the last few riders, then slowed to a walk next to Lydia and Zach.

"What's the matter, Tess?" Lydia asked, peering worriedly at me. "Did something happen back there?"

"Yeah—what's up? You look kind of weird," Zach added.

"I *feel* kind of weird," I said. "The strangest thing just happened!"

Very quietly, so none of the other riders could hear, I told Lydia and Zach about Joanna Talley's sudden appearance and what she had said to me.

"Joanna Talley, huh?" Zach whistled. "She's supposed to be a real dragon lady. Wonder what she's doing so far from home? Greenbriar's way on the other side of the river."

"And what did she mean by 'enemies'?" Lydia asked. "You don't think she was talking about the bikers or Old Man Putnam and his sons, do you?"

"She couldn't possibly know about them," I said. "Maybe she was just trying to scare me once she found out who I was. According to my parents, she doesn't like Matthew or any of the Sherrills very much."

Zach nodded. "Yeah, I know. Folks around here

say she really has it in for Matthew because he blew the whistle on her dad. My mom says she heard that Joanna Talley even blames him for the heart attack that carried old Mr. Talley off."

"Come to think of it, I wonder . . ." I began, then broke off. "No, forget it."

Zach glanced at me. "What were you going to say?"

I hesitated, then said slowly, "Well, I was just thinking that it's a heck of a coincidence, her showing up in the woods like that after the shots were fired."

Lydia gasped. "You mean she might have fired them herself? Oh, wow! Tess, are you going to tell Matthew about this?"

I thought about it for a minute, then shook my head. "Not right away. He's had enough worries for one night. I'll tell him tomorrow, after we've all had a good night's sleep."

But neither Matthew, Lydia, nor I had a good night's sleep.

It must have been about three o'clock in the morning when I sat bolt upright in bed. The dogs were barking like crazy. I threw off the covers and ran to the window.

"What's up?" Lydia mumbled groggily. "Tess? Where are you? What's all that noise?"

"It's Nemo and Flash," I told her, struggling to pull up the sash. "Something's wrong!"

Lydia scurried to my side, and we both stuck our

102

heads out, trying to see what the dogs were so excited about. At first we didn't see anything unusual. Then suddenly there were horses everywhere, galloping in all directions! The moonlight gleamed on a golden coat and a flowing, silvery mane and tail. *Ariel!*

"Somebody must have let them out!" I cried. "We've got to bring them back!"

~8~

I shoved my bare feet into my boots, threw on my windbreaker over my pajamas, and raced out the door, almost bumping into Matthew, who was coming out of his room across the hall. He was fully dressed—maybe he'd slept in his clothes. Neither of us said a word. We just pounded down the stairs as fast as we could and out into the cold, clear night, with Lydia a few paces behind.

"Here comes Lucky," she said, as the bay gelding trotted around the corner of the barn. "I'll try to head him off!"

Matthew's long legs had carried him almost to the stable yard by now, where Flash and Nemo were still barking frantically. I was right behind him, and I could see more horses pouring out of the barn.

"Shut the gate on this side, Tess!" Matthew called

105

over his shoulder. "I'll close the other one. Then get me a bridle—I'm going to ride out and try to find the rest of them."

We shut the gates barely in time to trap the horses inside. There must have been about a dozen of them, including Moonshine and Matthew's black gelding, Othello. Dodging flying hooves, I raced to the tack room, jammed a riding helmet on my head, snatched two bridles and a saddle, and ran back outside. Tossing one of the bridles to my uncle, I swiftly saddled and bridled the first horse I could catch, a roan named Sandy. Matthew was an excellent bareback rider, but I wasn't, and there was no way I was going to be left behind. I was sure he'd try to stop me if he knew what I had in mind, so I was glad that the confusion in the stable yard hid me from his sight until I had mounted.

"What do you think you're doing?" Matthew shouted when he saw me.

Setting my jaw, I said, "I'm coming with you."

"Oh no you're not! You're staying right here!"

I'd never argued with my uncle before, but this time I had to, for the palomino's sake. "You'll never be able to do it all by yourself," I cried. "Ariel's out there somewhere. She's probably frightened—maybe she's injured! I have to find her, I just have to! *Please*, Matthew!"

Before he could reply, Lydia opened the near gate wide enough to lead Lucky and another horse in, quickly latching it behind her. "I found Jupiter, too," she announced. "Anything else I can do to help?"

After a brief pause Matthew said, "Yes, there is. Call the sheriff's office and tell them what's happened. Ask them to send someone out here right away. Then see if you can get these horses back into their stalls, and until the police show up, keep the dogs with you. Tie them if you have to, but don't let them follow us." He glanced at me. "Tess and I are going to search for the others."

"Thanks," I said softly. "Oh, Matthew, thank you!"

Lydia let us out, and a moment later we were cantering the black gelding and the roan down the road. All I could think about was Ariel. I was pretty sure that some of the horses would make their way back to the stable on their own, but this was still foreign territory to the palomino mare. Masses of clouds were beginning to dim the moon's bright face. Even in broad daylight, the rock-studded fields and deep, hidden ravines could be dangerous to a running horse, especially one as delicately boned as Ariel.

Please let her be all right, I silently repeated over and over. *Please let me find her and bring her safely home!*

When we reached the end of the road, Matthew and I went in opposite directions. He rode along the shoulder of Route 22, and I began searching the fields nearby. There was hardly any moonlight now, and an early-morning mist made it even more difficult to see. I rode very slowly and carefully, straining for sight or sound of the missing horses.

At last two large shapes materialized out of the mist around the pond, whickering a greeting. Sandy neighed in reply, and I held my breath, hoping one of them might be Ariel. But when they came closer, I could tell even in what little light there was that neither had a golden coat or a quicksilver mane. I turned Sandy back to the barn, and the two horses trotted along on either side of us, more than willing to trade a brief taste of freedom for their familiar stalls.

As we approached the brightly lit stable yard, I saw Nemo and Flash tied to the fence. They heard us coming and began to bark. To my amazement, Zach ran out of the barn and opened the gate. He seized the halters of the other horses and led them inside, answering my question before I had a chance to ask it.

"Lydia called me right after she phoned the cops," he said. "She figured you and Matthew could use another hand."

"Could we ever!" I said. "Has my uncle come back yet?"

"He rode in a few minutes ago with three more horses. One of them's in pretty bad shape. Not Ariel," he added quickly, as though he had read my mind. "He hasn't found her yet. It's Mrs. Bronson's black gelding. Matthew thinks there's something really wrong with Midnight's shoulder—maybe a fracture."

"Oh, no," I whispered. I knew that in horses, a shoulder fracture was one of the few injuries that were impossible to treat. A horse with a broken shoulder blade almost always had to be destroyed.

"Matthew just called the vet, and Doc Ryan's on her way," Zach told me. "She'll take Midnight to her clinic for X-rays and stuff. Who knows? It might be only a muscle strain."

"I sure hope so! Where's Matthew now?" I asked.

Zach jerked his thumb in the direction of the office. "In there, with a couple of sheriff's deputies. He and Lydia have been telling them about what's been going on here lately, not just about the horses' being let out. The bikers, the graffiti, the gunshots—everything. They're going to stay here until the sheriff sends somebody to relieve them, just in case something else happens."

While he spoke, the horses he was holding had been moving restlessly and pawing the ground, eager to go into the stable. "I'm going to put these guys to bed," Zach said. "Stay here until I get back, okay? I'll saddle up Moonshine, and then we'll go after the rest of them." He started leading them to the stable door, then turned back. "Don't worry, Tess," he said gently. "We'll find her."

For the next couple of hours, Zach and I combed every inch of land for about a mile on both sides of the highway, coming back several times with the horses we found. Cinnamon's knees were scraped, and Lester, one of the boarders, was limping a little. Lady seemed to be all right, though, and so did the two horses that had wandered back by themselves. Only the palomino was still missing.

Doc Ryan had taken Midnight to the veterinary clinic while we were gone, leaving her associate, Dr. Pulanski, with Matthew to treat the less seriously injured horses and to examine the others. I couldn't forget the possibility that Midnight might have to be put down. And if Ariel was so badly hurt that she couldn't recover . . . *No!* I refused to think about it even for a second.

The harvest moon had set, and a gray, sullen dawn was breaking as Zach and I rode out again. This time we went farther than we ever had before, picking our way around granite boulders and fording a rushing stream that cut deeply through a stand of tall, dark evergreens. When we scrambled up the rocky bank on the other side, we were on the edge of a clearing. From the skeleton of a barn and a few jagged remnants of farm machinery, I knew the place had been abandoned for a long, long time.

"Nothing here," Zach said as we walked our horses across the field. "Tess, maybe we ought to go back. We can look for Ariel later, after we've had some rest."

I was so tired that I could hardly stay upright in the saddle, and my teeth were chattering from the cold, but I shook my head. "You go back if you want to. I'm not giving up, not yet. Not ever!"

Suddenly Moonshine raised his head and let out a high, piercing whinny. From somewhere—maybe from inside what was left of the barn—I heard an answering neigh.

Zach and I stared at each other. Then we urged our mounts into a canter. I reached the barn first, and slid to the ground just as a small gold-and-silver horse trotted awkwardly between the timbers that had once supported a door.

"Ariel!" I shouted, stumbling toward her. "Zach, it's Ariel! Moonshine found her!"

I threw my arms around the mare's neck, tears of exhaustion and relief running down my cheeks. After a moment I felt Zach's hands on my shoulders, gently pulling me away.

"Listen, Tess," he said urgently. "We've found her, but we have to get her to the vet pronto. She's hurt."

That's when I really looked at Ariel for the first time and saw the jagged tear that ran down her side to her left flank. In the early-morning light, the blood that stained her golden coat looked black.

I cried out and clung to Zach, burying my face in his denim jacket and choking on great, gasping sobs. If he hadn't held me close, my trembling legs probably would have given way beneath me.

"She must have run into something in the dark—maybe that rusty old cultivator over there," Zach

111

said. "The sooner Dr. Pulanski or Doc Ryan can take care of her, the better."

"What if—what if she's hurt inside?" I mumbled against his chest when I was finally able to speak. I couldn't bear to look at Ariel and see that awful wound again. "The stable's so far away. What if she bleeds to death on the way?"

Zach grasped my chin firmly with one hand and raised my face until his eyes met mine. "I don't think it's as bad as it looks, Tess, honest. Anyway, we can't just leave her here. We have to try to bring her back. We'll take it real easy—I'm pretty sure there's a bridge over that stream we crossed." He took a lead line out of the pocket of his jacket. "Want me to lead her?"

I wiped my streaming eyes and runny nose on my sleeve and shook my head. "No. No, I'll do it."

Taking the line, I walked over to where the palomino stood patiently next to Moonshine and Sandy and fastened it to her halter. "Come on, girl," I whispered, stroking her soft nose. "We're going home."

I'm not sure how long it took us to make the return trip to The Barn. All I know is that by the time Zach and I rode into the stable yard with Ariel following me on her lead, the sun wasn't shining but the sky was light. The last thing I remember is slipping out of Sandy's saddle into Matthew's arms. Zach told me later that I kept saying, "She didn't die! Ariel *didn't* die! Don't let them kill her!" I was so exhausted that I guess I got Ariel and Midnight all mixed up in my mind.

Matthew must have carried me to the house, because when I finally woke up, I was snuggled in bed beneath the patchwork quilt. It took me a few minutes to figure out where I was. As soon as I did, everything came back to me in a rush. I sat bolt upright, brushing my tangled hair out of my eyes.

"Morning, sleepyhead," Lydia said. She was sitting in the rocking chair by the window, peering solemnly at me through her glasses. "Or maybe I should say good afternoon—it's almost one o'clock. How are you feeling?"

"I'm not sure . . ." I stretched my arms over my head and winced. All those hours in the saddle had left every muscle in my body aching something fierce. "Stiff as a board, but I guess I'll live. What about Ariel? Have you heard how she's doing?" I asked anxiously. "What did the vet say? Is she going to be okay? Is she at Doc Ryan's clinic or is she still here?"

"Whoa! Slow down," Lydia exclaimed, laughing. "One question at a time!"

I made a zipping motion across my mouth, and she nodded. "That's better. Okay, here goes. I was falling asleep on my feet, so Matthew made me go to bed before you brought her back. But he told me a little while ago that he and Dr. Pulanski took Ariel to the clinic, and Doc Ryan checked her out right away.

113

She's going to be okay, Tess—the cut isn't all that deep. Both vets say it should heal just fine, but nobody will be able to ride her for a while, and she'll probably always have a scar."

Though I hated the thought of the palomino's being scarred for life, she would always be the most beautiful, perfect horse in the world to me. And I was ecstatic that Ariel hadn't been as badly injured as I'd feared. I was also thinking that even if Mr. Graham sent for her right away, she wouldn't be able to make the long trip to New Jersey for some time yet, not until she was fully recovered. I flopped back on my pillows, letting out a huge sigh of relief. Then suddenly I remembered the black gelding.

Propping myself up on one elbow, I asked, "What about Midnight?"

Lydia's smile faded and she avoided my eyes, looking down at the rag rug under her feet. "Doc Ryan called Matthew a couple of hours ago. She said it's a shoulder fracture. It's hopeless—there's nothing she or anybody else can do. Once Mrs. Bronson gives her permission, Doc Ryan will . . ." Lydia shivered. "You know what she'll have to do."

"Oh, how horrible," I murmured, a lump in my throat. "Poor Midnight! And poor Mrs. Bronson! Has Matthew told her yet?"

"He went to her house as soon as he got off the phone with the vet. I heard him talking to Zach when he got back." Lydia hesitated, then went on.

114

"Mrs. Bronson was really furious. She blames Matthew for what happened to Midnight, and she said she's going to tell all the other people who board their horses at The Barn to take them somewhere else."

I couldn't believe my ears. "You've got to be kidding! She was probably so upset that she didn't know what she was saying. She would never do a thing like that—Midnight has boarded here for years, and Mrs. Bronson's told me dozens of times how pleased she is with the way Matthew cares for all the horses. She wouldn't want to ruin his reputation. When she calms down, she'll realize that it wasn't his fault."

"I sure hope so," Lydia said. "I guess Matthew would lose a lot of money if the boarders left. And anyway, if she *did* convince some of them to leave, where would they go?"

Her question echoed in my head. *Where would they go? Where would they go?* Suddenly all the scary things that had taken place over the past few weeks formed a pattern, and I was sure I knew exactly where they would go.

"Of course!" I shouted, throwing off the covers and leaping out of bed. "That's what she was doing in the woods last night! And she must have let the horses out too!"

Lydia was staring at me as if I'd lost my mind. "What do you mean? Who are you talking about?"

"Joanna Talley! I bet she graffitied the stable as a kind of warning, first. Then she fired those shots during the trail ride and rode over here later, after we were all asleep, and chased the horses out. She had to know that some of them were bound to be injured, and she probably figures that pretty soon people will decide The Barn's a dangerous place. The renters will stop coming, the boarders will move their horses to Greenbriar, and Matthew will go out of business. And if Mrs. Bronson makes a big fuss, it'll happen *very* soon!"

"Wow!" Lydia said. "You really think Joanna Talley hates him that much?"

"You heard what Zach said last night about her blaming Matthew for her father's heart attack. I bet she's been plotting her revenge ever since he died."

Lydia shivered. "If that's true, she really *is* a dragon lady! You'd better tell Sheriff Griswold right away!"

My shoulders slumped and I sat back down on the bed. "Tell him what? That I *think* she did all that stuff? He'd be sure to ask for evidence, and I don't have any, not really. I could tell him about meeting her near the woods last night, but it's not a crime to ride your own horse in a public place."

"Then what are you going to do?" Lydia asked.

"I'm not sure," I admitted. "Right now I'm going to take a shower." I looked down at the grungy pajamas I was wearing and made a face. "I'll be able to think better when I'm clean and wearing real clothes.''

Maybe the hot water and a change of clothing actually did help to clear my head. Anyway, by the time I came downstairs, in my sweatshirt, jeans, and boots, I'd decided what I had to do. I told Lydia and Zach about it in the kitchen while Zach and I wolfed down the mountains of scrambled eggs and tons of toast Lydia had prepared.

Matthew wasn't there. According to Zach, he was at the stable, dealing with reporters from the Stockton *Times* and trying to convince several worried owners not to remove their horses from The Barn—now that Midnight had been destroyed, Mrs. Bronson had made good on her threat.

"You're nuts," Zach said when I had finished describing my plan. "Going to Greenbriar and snooping around isn't going to prove anything. To begin with, if she *did* do it—and I don't think she did—Joanna Talley's not dumb enough to leave incriminating evidence lying around.''

"And what if she catches you? She could have you arrested for trespassing or something," Lydia added. "I don't think it's a good idea, Tess.''

"Thanks for the support, guys," I said wryly, slathering butter on my fourth piece of toast.

"The way I see it, you've got it all wrong," Zach argued. "Joanna Talley may have a motive for wanting to give Matthew a hard time, but she's not the only one. My money's on the bikers. They're not the type to make threats and then not carry them out."

I suddenly remembered the sound I thought I'd heard last night just after the gunshots. It could have been a motorcycle engine, but it could also have been the drone of a distant plane.

"What about the Putnams?" Lydia said, pouring more orange juice into our glasses. "They have a *really* strong motive—greed! If Matthew was forced out of business, he'd have to sell his property to Mr. Brewster. Then Mr. Brewster would buy Old Man Putnam's farm, and those three nasty people would be rich."

Her green eyes widened, and I got the feeling that she was about to come up with one of her bizarre theories. I was right. "Then there's Mr. Brewster himself!" she cried. "Maybe he's behind the whole thing! He could have bribed Joanna Talley or somebody else to do his dirty work for him. You know how badly he wants Matthew to sell this land to him."

Zach sighed. "I doubt Mr. Brewster would do something like that, Lydia, but I guess we have to consider all the possibilities." He turned to me. "Tess, you're going to have to tell your folks about this when you go home tonight. Maybe you ought to tell them about our suspicions, too. They might be able to help us decide what to do."

I had almost forgotten that I'd be going home in a few hours. Now that Zach had reminded me, my heart sank. He was right—there was no way I could avoid telling Mom and Dad about everything that had been happening at The Barn. I had a pretty good idea of what their reaction would be, and I wasn't looking forward to it.

~9~

Zach dropped me off at my house at about six o'clock that evening, after he'd driven Lydia home. He had offered to give us a lift because, he said, we both looked beat. I guess Zach was pretty beat himself—he couldn't have had more than a couple of hours of sleep on the sofa in Matthew's living room, and I don't think Matthew had slept at all.

"Call me tomorrow, Tess, and let me know what your folks have to say," he told me as I got out of his beat-up old car. "And get some rest, okay?"

"I will," I said. "You rest up too. And Zach . . ."

"Yeah?"

I hesitated, feeling suddenly shy as I remembered the way I'd cried all over him that morning. He'd been awfully nice to me then, even though he was kind of obnoxious when I told him my theory about

Joanna Talley. "Thanks for everything," I mumbled. "Coming back last night, I mean, and helping to find Ariel, and bringing Lydia and me home, and—well, everything."

I was pretty sure I saw him blush. "No problem," he said. With that he gunned the motor and shifted gears with a screech that made me cringe.

I watched as the battered green sedan chugged down Brookfield Street and turned the corner, then walked slowly up the path to my front door. My father's car wasn't in the driveway, so I knew that my parents and Sabrina hadn't returned yet. I couldn't help hoping they'd be very late. If they came back after I was in bed, I wouldn't have to tell them all the details until the next morning.

But I realized that by then they would most likely have seen the Stockton *Times*, and I decided that no matter how tired I was, I had to tell my family what had happened before they read about it in the paper and freaked out. At least I could give them an eye-witness account instead of some reporter's second-hand version.

My parents and Sabrina got home about an hour after I did, and the minute they walked in the door, I sat them down in the living room and told them the whole story.

". . . And no matter what Mrs. Bronson says, it *wasn't* Matthew's fault that Midnight had to be put down," I finished.

I was afraid they'd be angry, and they were, but not at Matthew.

"This is an outrage!" my usually soft-spoken father bellowed. "It's obvious that somebody is trying to destroy my brother's livelihood, and I won't stand for it."

"I certainly don't approve of Matthew's lifestyle, but this kind of harassment is intolerable," my mother agreed. "The nerve of Carla Bronson! I always knew she was a difficult woman, but I never thought she'd be vindictive."

My father stood up. "I'm going to call Jack Griswold immediately. I want a full-scale investigation into this matter, beginning first thing tomorrow morning."

"But, Dad, it's Sunday night. Sheriff Griswold probably won't be in his office," Sabrina pointed out.

"I'll call him at home—his number's in my book. And then I'm going to phone Matthew. He's never accepted my help before, but this time I'm not going to take no for an answer!"

While Dad made the calls in his study, Mom, Sabrina, and I fixed a makeshift supper of leftovers and frozen pizza. It wasn't one of my mom's better meals, but I don't think any of us noticed what we were eating—I know I didn't.

Though I was still very upset, I was glad that for once my whole family was on the same side. And I was also glad that my parents hadn't forbidden me to go to The Barn. I have to admit that I'd kind of played down my part in the events of the previous night when I told them about it. I didn't want them to think I'd been in danger. Maybe it wasn't exactly honest, but it wasn't a lie, either. As far as I was concerned, I *wasn't* in any danger—Ariel and the other horses were, and that was the only thing that mattered.

But as we sat around the kitchen table, I did tell them about who Lydia, Zach, and I thought the culprits might be, figuring that Dad could pass along our suspicions to Sheriff Griswold. To say the least, they weren't very impressed, particularly when I mentioned Joanna Talley.

Mom gave me a sympathetic look and patted my hand. "Tess dear, I really don't think Ms. Talley would become involved in criminal mischief, no matter how strongly she resents Matthew. I think your imagination was working overtime after the terrifying experience you had."

My father nodded. "Jack Griswold assured me that Matthew has given him all the information he needs to investigate the case, and I told Matthew that I'm going out to his place tomorrow morning to discuss how I can be of assistance. Don't worry about it, honey. We'll take care of everything."

"We know you want to help, Tess, but let the authorities handle it," my mother said firmly. "Now run along upstairs, have a nice hot bath, and go straight to bed. You have to get up for school tomorrow."

124

I didn't argue. A hot bath and bed sounded pretty good to me. But before I collapsed, there was one more thing I had to do. Going into Dad's study, I looked up Doc Ryan's veterinary clinic in the phone book and dialed the number. The vet herself answered.

"Hello, Dr. Ryan? This is Tess Sherrill, Matthew Sherrill's niece," I said. "I'm sorry to disturb you, but I was wondering if you can tell me how Ariel's doing—she's the palomino who was injured this morning," I added in case Doc Ryan didn't know Ariel's name.

"Oh, hello, Tess. Ariel's in pretty good shape, all things considered," Doc Ryan said. She sounded as tired as I felt. "Fortunately, the lacerations weren't very deep. No muscles or major vessels were severed, so she didn't lose too much blood. But she's still fairly weak and quite groggy—we had to give her general anesthesia in order to cleanse and suture the wound. If her temperature remains normal and there are no signs of infection, your uncle should be able to take her back to The Barn on Wednesday."

"That's great!" I cried. "Would it be all right if I came out to visit her tomorrow? I could come right after school."

"I'm afraid not," the vet said regretfully. "I don't allow my surgical patients to have visitors. Though the mare's doing well, she needs complete rest and quiet to recover from both the physical and emotional trauma she's suffered. I'm sorry, Tess—

Matthew told me how fond you are of Ariel, and I know how much you want to see her. But rest assured that your horse is receiving the very best care Dr. Pulanski and I can provide. She's going to be just fine, and in time the scar will hardly be noticeable." She sighed wearily. "I only wish we could be as successful with every sick or injured animal that's brought to us for help."

I knew she was thinking about Midnight, and though I was disappointed at not being allowed to visit Ariel, I was reminded again of how much worse her injury might have been. Compared to never seeing the palomino again, three days wasn't too long to wait.

The next day at school, everybody was talking about the events at The Barn. Stockton's such a quiet little town most of the time that a Cub Scout outing is considered big news, so it's no wonder the article about it made the front page of the *Times*, along with a big picture of Matthew and some of his horses in front of the stable. The banner headline made me cringe: SHERRILL STABLE VANDALIZED, GUNSHOTS FIRED, HORSES INJURED.

Neither Lydia's name nor mine was mentioned, but all our friends knew we spent a lot of time there, and everyone knew that Matthew was my uncle. Some of the kids also knew that we had gone on the Harvest Moon Trail Ride, and they wanted to hear all the gory details. Though Lydia and I did our best to make it seem like it was no big deal, I don't think many of them were convinced. Rebecca Platt, one of the members of the volleyball team, certainly wasn't.

"My boyfriend and I were going to rent a couple of your uncle's horses next weekend," she whispered to me in French class, "but we changed our minds. I mean, horseback riding's kind of dangerous anyway, and what with everything that's been going on out there—well, we decided to go to the movies instead."

Even the teachers were gossiping about the situation. I was standing next to the open door of the faculty lounge at lunchtime, waiting for Lydia, who was late as usual, when I heard Mr. Domanic, my English teacher, saying, "In my opinion, there's some kind of vendetta against Matthew Sherrill, and I can't understand it. I don't know the man personally, but his niece Theresa is one of my best students, and she seems to think very highly of him."

"*Nobody* knows Sherrill personally," another man said. "From what I hear, he's the black sheep of that family. Who knows what kind of trouble he's gotten himself into or what enemies he's made?"

"Some friends of mine were on that trail ride." I recognized the high, nasal voice of Ms. Campbell, my French teacher. "They said it was absolutely terrifying! The entire area was sprayed with gunfire. I wouldn't ride there if you paid me."

A second woman added, "It wasn't in the paper, but my cousin knows someone who works at the animal hospital, and he told me that one of the horses was shot and had to be destroyed!"

I gritted my teeth and clenched my fists. It's a good thing that Lydia came along just then, or I probably would have marched into the lounge and given them a piece of my mind, teachers or no teachers—except Mr. Domanic. He was okay.

"What's the matter, Tess?" Lydia asked. "I can almost see the steam pouring out of your ears. Why are you so mad?"

As we hurried down the hall to the cafeteria, I told her what the teachers had been saying. "This could really hurt Matthew, you know."

"Oh, Tess, don't worry so much," Lydia said. "Once we find out who's responsible for all the trouble, everything will be fine. But you know what? When Jeremy walked me to biology this morning, he said he was worried about me. He doesn't think I ought to go out to The Barn anymore, at least until they lock up the perpetrator."

It took me a second to remember that Jeremy was an editor on the school paper, the guy Lydia said was almost as cute as Zach but not quite. "Well, I hope he's not going to write an article about this," I said, frowning. "All Matthew needs is more bad publicity!"

"He won't," Lydia assured me. "Tess, would you stop worrying! Anyway, he's taking me out for a soda after the staff meeting this afternoon. Jeremy says that as long as I'm with him, he knows I'm okay. Isn't that sweet?"

She drifted through the doorway to the cafeteria, obviously more interested in her date with Jeremy than in Matthew's troubles. I wondered if she had lost interest in Zach, but I wasn't about to ask her. I was a little annoyed that she had let Jeremy believe that my uncle's stable was dangerous, but I guess love does strange things to people.

Well, Lydia might have forgotten Matthew's problems, but for the rest of the day, I couldn't think about anything else. In spite of what my parents had said about letting the sheriff's department handle the investigation, I couldn't just sit around while Sheriff Griswold and his men searched for the culprits. It might take weeks, maybe even months, and now it was more urgent than ever to solve the mystery before people stopped coming to The Barn altogether.

Since there was nothing I could do for Ariel, I decided to check out Greenbriar Stables after school, hoping to find some evidence that would prove Joanna Talley's guilt. I wouldn't even have to go home and change, because I was wearing jeans and boots—designer jeans and kind of dressy boots, but I'd be able to ride in them.

As soon as the final bell rang, I raced to my locker, tossed the books I'd need for homework into my backpack, and pulled on my heavy cable-knit sweater. I made it to the bus stop just in time. When I climbed on board and dropped my money into the slot, one of the passengers peered at me and said, "You're related to that Matthew Sherrill, right? The guy that was written up in the paper?"

"Yes, I am," I said. "Matthew Sherrill's my uncle." Everyone within earshot stared at me as if I was some kind of celebrity—or maybe some kind of freak.

As I made my way down the aisle to an empty seat, an elderly woman reached out and tugged at the sleeve of my sweater. "That was a terrible thing that happened at your uncle's stable," she said, shaking her head. "A terrible thing! I heard that four riders were shot, and two horses were hit by cars and killed right on this very road. I simply can't understand how Mr. Sherrill could have allowed it to happen!"

Very politely but very loudly so everybody could hear, I said, "Excuse me, ma'am, but you heard wrong. *No* riders were shot, and *none* of the horses were hit by cars. And as for what actually did happen, it wasn't my uncle's fault. Take my word for it —I was there."

"Well, you shouldn't have been," the old lady snapped. "A child like you should have been home in bed where you belonged. In *my* day . . ."

I didn't wait to hear about her day. As I sank into an aisle seat as far away from her as possible, the elderly man next to me smiled and said, "Don't you pay any attention to Flora Jessup. She's always got some kinda bee in her bonnet. Thinks she knows

130

everything, and she don't hesitate to say so." He added, "I'm real sorry about all Matthew's troubles, and you can tell him I said so. Tell him Frank and Martha Trumbull send him their best regards, and if there's anything we can do to help, all he has to do is call."

"Thanks, Mr. Trumbull," I said. "He'll be happy to hear it. Matthew buys all his butter and eggs from your wife, doesn't he? I had some of her bread and cookies the other day too. They were delicious."

"Butter and eggs, yes. But Martha don't bake anymore," Mr. Trumbull told me. "You must be thinking about somebody else."

Here's another mystery, I thought. If Mrs. Trumbull hadn't baked that bread and those cookies, who did? Maybe Lydia was right. Maybe there *was* a woman in my uncle's life, someone a lot younger than Martha Trumbull. But who could it possibly be?

I wondered about that for the rest of the trip. I probably would have missed my stop if Mr. Trumbull hadn't told me we were approaching The Barn.

"Thanks, Mr. Trumbull," I said as I stood up. "It was nice talking to you. I'll be sure to give Matthew your message."

"You do that," the old man said as I headed for the door. "Take care now."

Walking down the road toward the stable, I saw a brown-and-white police car in the parking area near Matthew's truck and Zach's and Orville's cars. The only person in sight was a man in a deputy's uniform throwing sticks for Nemo and Flash to fetch. When the dogs saw me, they galloped over to say hello, then scampered back to pick up their game where they had left off. I guess I didn't look very threatening, because after one quick glance, the deputy paid no attention to me at all.

I went into the stable yard, calling, "Matthew? Zach? Orville? Anybody home?" but there was no reply. *Where is everybody?* I wondered as I stepped inside and walked slowly down the aisle between the stalls. Horses poked their heads out over the doors, greeting me with an occasional snort or a whinny, but several stalls were empty: Ariel's and Midnight's, of course—I averted my eyes from his loose box with a shiver—and four boarders'. Othello's stall was empty too, I noticed.

Just then I heard the sound of booted feet clumping down the wooden stairs from the upper level of the barn, and Zach appeared.

"Oh, uh, hi, Tess," he said, obviously surprised to see me there on a weekday. "Gee, you look—different. Guess I never saw you wearing nice clothes. . . ." He blushed. "I mean, the stuff you usually wear— I mean—well, you look nice."

I felt my face flushing. "Thanks. These are just my regular clothes. I came out here right after school." I almost told him what I had in mind, but then I decided against it because I was pretty sure he'd try to talk me out of it. "I just thought I'd see how things were doing—maybe go for a little ride. Did Matthew take Othello out?"

"Yeah. He left about a half hour ago. Orville and I have been working upstairs. What horse do you want?"

I thought for a moment. "Lucky, I guess. I've been feeling a little guilty about neglecting him since Ariel arrived. Here's my chance to make it up to him. I'll probably be riding him until Ariel's fit again."

"I'll help you tack him up," Zach said. As we walked together to the tack room, he added, "Matthew talked to Doc Ryan today. She says Ariel's doing real well, and she'll probably be coming home day after tomorrow."

"I know," I said, putting on my hard hat. "I called her last night and she told me the same thing. I wanted to visit Ariel today, but Doc Ryan wouldn't let me. So I decided to come out here instead." I found Lucky's bridle and hurried to his stall.

Zach followed me with the saddle. "What's the rush?" he asked as I slipped the bit between Lucky's big yellow teeth and quickly fastened the throat latch.

"No rush exactly," I said not quite truthfully, "but I don't want to be too late getting home. By the way, my parents are behind Matthew one hundred percent." That part was definitely true. "Dad even came out here this morning to talk to him and find out if there's anything he can do to help. And I sure hope

133

there is, because you wouldn't believe the rumors that are going around Stockton!"

Zach had fastened and tested the girth of Lucky's saddle, and now I led him out of his stall. Zach gave me a leg up and I gathered the reins. "Well, see you in a little while," I said, nudging the gelding with my heels.

"If you run into Matthew, the two of you could ride together," Zach called after me as Lucky and I trotted out of the stable. "Not that I think there's any danger, but . . ."

"Don't worry," I called back. "I'll be fine."

I kept Lucky to a trot until we turned onto the dirt road on the other side of the pond. When I knew the trees would screen us from Zach's view, I gave the gelding his head and urged him into an easy lope. We had a lot of ground to cover between The Barn and Greenbriar Stables. I sure hoped we wouldn't meet Matthew along the way, because if we did, I'd have to put off my scouting expedition until another day, and there wasn't any time to lose.

Even though I was in a big hurry, I didn't want to push Lucky too hard, so we'd canter a little, then trot for a while, and walk for a few minutes. While we were walking, I savored the beauty of the afternoon. Beneath a brilliant blue sky, the mountains glowed in their full autumn glory of red, russet, and gold. Even the woods that had seemed so dark and scary on Saturday night were golden and welcoming in the slanting sunlight.

In less than an hour, Lucky and I were trotting along the shoulder of the narrow blacktop that ran past Joanna Talley's place. Greenbriar Stables lay in a broad valley surrounded by gently rolling hills. A few horses grazed in one of the white-fenced paddocks, but the others were empty. I reined Lucky to a halt, trying to recognize any of the horses, but none of them looked familiar. If Matthew's boarders had transferred their mounts to Greenbriar, they had to be inside the stable building.

I walked the bay down the road until we came to a gravel drive that led to the stable entrance. I didn't see anybody around. Glancing at the sprawling stone house not far away, I didn't see any signs of life there, either. Except for a flight of barn swallows swooping overhead and the horses in the field, the dragon lady's lair seemed deserted.

"Well, here goes," I murmured to Lucky, patting his shoulder. I walked him down the drive and dismounted, looping his reins around an old-fashioned hitching post next to the wide double doors. Lucky whuffled softly and began nibbling at some of the sparse grass around the post. Taking a deep breath, I tiptoed inside.

The first thing I saw made me stop in my tracks. Othello was tethered not far from the entrance! When he saw me, he raised his head and whickered a greeting.

"What on earth are *you* doing here?" I whispered.

And then it came to me. Matthew must have had

the same suspicions about Joanna Talley that I did, and he'd decided to confront her on her own turf. Had he found her? If he had, maybe he could use some reinforcements.

I looked around, trying to figure out where the two of them might be. Seeing a couple of doors to my right, I ran over and flung open one of them, discovering only an empty feed room. Pausing outside the second door, I heard voices inside—my uncle's and a woman's. I opened the door a crack and peeked inside. It was a tack room, and what I saw really blew my mind!

Matthew was standing there with his arms around a woman with long, honey-blond hair. I guess I must have made some kind of startled squeak, because they turned toward the door. I saw that the woman was really beautiful, and when she spoke, I recognized her voice immediately. It was the same voice I'd heard on the night of the trail ride on the road by the woods.

"Well, hello, Theresa Sherrill," she said. "We've met before. I'm Joanna Talley, and your uncle and I have some wonderful news. We're going to be married."

⌐10⌐

"You're *what*?" I gasped, staring from Joanna Talley's smiling face to Matthew's.

Though I was totally stunned at seeing the two of
them, for some reason neither of them seemed very
surprised to see me. It was almost as if they'd been
expecting me. But that was impossible. I hadn't told
anyone where I was going, not even Lydia.

"You heard the lady, Tess," Matthew said, one
arm still around the blond woman's slim waist.
There were dark circles under his eyes and he looked
awfully tired, but he also looked happy. "We're going to be married. I know you think Joanna's one of
the bad guys, but she's really a pretty nice person."
She glared at him in mock indignation, and Matthew's smile broadened as he corrected himself. "A

very nice person, as you'll find out when you get to know her. You liked her bread, remember?"

I was having a hard time taking this all in. *"You're* the mystery baker?" I said to Joanna Talley in what I hoped was something like my normal voice. "The bread and the cookies, too?"

She nodded. "The bread and the cookies, too. I'm glad you enjoyed them, Theresa."

"Oh, wow!" I whispered. I guess I was a little slow on the uptake, because it took a minute for the rest of what Matthew had said to sink in. When it did, I turned to my uncle. "Wh-what did you mean about my thinking Ms. Talley was one of the bad guys?" I stammered. "H-how did you know?"

"Your father mentioned it when he came to The Barn this morning," Matthew said, his dark eyes twinkling with amusement. "He also told me about the names Zach and Lydia added to your most-wanted list, but apparently Joanna's was at the top. I was pretty sure you'd come here sooner or later to check up on her, and I'm glad you decided to do it on the day Joanna promised to be my wife. You can help us celebrate."

Of all the weird things that had happened lately, this was definitely the weirdest. My prime suspect was about to become my aunt! Some detective I was! I've never been so embarrassed in my life. My face felt like it was on fire.

I swallowed hard. "I'm really sorry, Ms. Talley," I

mumbled. "I didn't know—that is, I really thought— I mean . . ."

"It's perfectly all right," she said, smiling. "Actually, Theresa, I was kind of flattered. I don't think I've ever been at the top of anyone's list before . . ." She looked demurely at my uncle. "Except maybe Matthew's."

"Definitely Matthew's," Matthew said with a grin. Glancing over at me, he added, "But I warn you, Joanna, you'll have to share that honor with Tess. She's been there for almost fifteen years."

That made me feel so much better that I managed a smile of my own, even though I was still a little dazed.

Joanna Talley left Matthew's side and crossed the room to me. "Since we're going to be related, won't you please call me Joanna?" she said. "And may I call you Tess, the way your friends do? I'd really like to be your friend."

I shook the hand she extended to me, noticing that her grip was firm and strong. "I'd like that too," I replied softly, and I really meant it.

"Good!" Joanna said. "Now that we've got that settled, let's all go up to the house for that celebration Matthew mentioned." She grinned. "Since I wasn't expecting a proposal, I haven't prepared anything fancy, but I can offer you herb tea and some pumpkin bread I baked this morning. Do you like herb tea, Tess? I brew my own from the herbs I grow in my garden."

I nodded numbly. The dragon lady was into herb tea and pumpkin bread. Zach would never believe it! I could hardly believe it myself. As the three of us left the stable and walked to the house, my thoughts were churning. I still had a lot of questions, but I decided to wait until I could think more clearly before I put them into words.

Soon we were seated with our mugs of tea in Joanna's comfortable, slightly shabby living room. Matthew built a fire in the big stone fireplace, and two large, friendly cats made themselves at home in my lap and Joanna's.

"What did you mean the other night about Matthew having enemies?" I asked her after we had all sipped our tea and tasted the delicious pumpkin bread. "That really threw me for a loop."

Stroking the tiger-striped cat in her lap, Joanna said, "I'm sorry, Tess. I didn't mean to scare you, but I guess it must have sounded rather menacing. The fact is, I was worried about your uncle." She looked at Matthew. "First the graffiti and then the gunshots —well, it just seemed to me that they were somehow connected, and that someone meant to do you harm."

"As things turned out, it seems you were right," Matthew said ruefully.

Joanna turned back to me. "You thought I was one of those enemies, didn't you?"

"Yes," I admitted. Feeling more than a little

foolish, I told her and Matthew everything that had led me to that conclusion.

"I never blamed Matthew for my father's death, or for anything else," Joanna said. "Dad wasn't the easiest person in the world to live with. We didn't see eye to eye on a lot of things, including the way he treated his horses. What he called strict discipline seemed more like harsh punishment to me. But even though I was his partner in the business, I couldn't make him change his ways."

She paused for a moment, then went on. "We had a big argument about a year ago. I moved out, went to Virginia, and got a job as a trainer in a stable. I'd probably still be there if Dad's doctor hadn't called to tell me about his heart attack. I came back to take care of him—and Greenbriar, which was in pretty bad shape by then. It wasn't easy, but two good things happened. Before he died, Dad and I made up, and I met your uncle." Joanna and Matthew smiled at each other.

"Jo wasn't boycotting the store, Tess," Matthew said. "As I told your father today, she was away for a long time, and when she came home, she didn't have either the time or the money to spend in Sherrill's—or anywhere else, for that matter."

"But if all Matthew's boarders moved their horses to Greenbriar, then you *would* have money," I said to Joanna. "That's one of the reasons I thought—well, you know what I thought."

She nodded, smiling slightly. "Yes, I certainly do!

141

And several of them contacted me about stabling their horses here. I was so angry at those people for running out on Matthew that I almost turned them down, but he persuaded me to change my mind. He knew I'd give them the best of care, and it was the welfare of the horses that mattered, not my own personal feelings."

By now I realized that my suspicions of Joanna had been based mostly on what I'd heard other people say about her. And that meant I was just as bad as the people who made me so angry, the ones who believed every rumor they heard about Matthew. I was ashamed of myself, because Matthew was right —she *was* a nice person, and I decided I liked her a lot. I also liked her pumpkin bread, and so did the fat gray cat that was draped across my knees. Between us, we polished off two big slices while Matthew, Joanna, and I talked.

When the clock on the mantel chimed five times, it took me by surprise. Removing the cat from my lap, I stood up. "I really have to be going," I said. "I'd love to stay, but Zach will be wondering what's happened to me, and so will my parents if I'm late."

Matthew stood up too. "We'll ride back together, and then I'll drive you home. Your parents invited me to have supper with the family tonight."

"Oh, Matthew, I'm so glad!" I exclaimed.

Joanna smiled at my uncle. "So am I. It's very important for families to stick together, especially when there's trouble."

She walked with us to where we had left our horses. Before I mounted, she put her hands on my shoulders. Looking straight into my eyes, she said, "Friends?"

"Friends," I said.

When Matthew and I got back to The Barn, there wasn't enough time to tell Zach everything I'd learned, so as he helped me unsaddle Lucky, I just gave him the headline.

"Joanna Talley didn't do it," I said, "and that means somebody else did."

Zach stared at me. "How do you know? Geez, Tess, you didn't go to Greenbriar and *ask* the dragon lady, did you?"

"As a matter of fact, I did," I said, grinning. "That's where I found Matthew. And incidentally, Joanna's not a dragon lady. She's really nice, and she and Matthew are engaged to be married."

I thought Zach's eyes would pop right out of his head. "You're kidding! How—when—what—"

"Ask Matthew tomorrow," I said. "He'll give you all the details."

"Tess, you about ready?" my uncle called from the stable doorway.

"Coming," I called back. "Listen, Zach, I have to run—Matthew's driving me home. But I'll see you the day after tomorrow, when I come out to see Ariel. I'll see if Lydia can come too. Now that Joanna's not a suspect anymore, we have to figure out where we go from here."

I left him shaking his head and muttering, "Geez! Matthew and Joanna Talley!"

After supper that night, I called Lydia to tell her the latest news. Naturally she was thrilled.

"That's just about the most romantic thing I ever heard," she sighed. "I *knew* there was a woman in Matthew's life, but I never dreamed it was Joanna Talley!"

But when I asked her to come with me to The Barn on Wednesday, she hesitated. "Gosh, Tess, I'd like to, but—well, the drama club's starting rehearsals for their new production. Jeremy's vice president, and today he talked me into designing the costumes. I have to meet with him and the scene designer Wednesday after school, and then I told Jeremy I'd go out with him . . ."

". . . for a soda," I finished for her.

"For a burger, actually," Lydia said. "But how about Thursday?"

"I'll have to ask Zach. Thursday and Friday are his days off. Maybe he could meet us somewhere in town. I'll let you know, okay?"

"Okay." After a pause, Lydia asked, "You're not mad at me, are you, Tess? For not going with you to The Barn on Wednesday, I mean."

"No, silly, I'm not mad," I said. "I don't expect you to give up all your other activities until the mystery's solved. After all, Matthew's not *your* uncle."

"I know, but I like him a lot and I do want to help. It's just that—well, Jeremy's sort of special. In fact,

144

he's *very* special," she said. "Remember when I told you I thought I was in love with Zach? Well, I was wrong. I mean, Zach's gorgeous and everything, but we have absolutely nothing in common. With Jeremy it's the real thing, Tess. I'm sure of it!"

"I'm glad," I said, and I really was. But when we finally got off the phone, I couldn't help thinking that Lydia's new romance certainly was fouling up our detective work!

On Wednesday I could hardly wait to welcome Ariel home from the clinic. I asked Ms. Clifford, the volleyball coach, if I could leave practice a little early, and she said I could. I was so out of it that I'd been hitting the ball into the net every time it came my way, so I wasn't much of an asset to my team.

This time none of the other passengers on the bus had anything to say about the events at The Barn. It was the same way at school. Now that the story wasn't on the front page of the local paper, everybody seemed to have forgotten all about it. But I would never forget, and neither would Matthew and Joanna.

When I first saw Ariel that afternoon, it was all I could do to keep from bursting into tears. The hair on her left flank and side had been shaved around the area of the wound, and ugly black stitches held the edges of skin together.

"Can I—can I touch her?" I whispered to Matthew, who had come with me to the palomino's stall.

145

"Of course," he said. "Just steer clear of the sutures. Ariel's going to be all right, Tess, she really is. Doc Ryan says she's healing beautifully, and the stitches can come out in about a week. From then on, it's up to Mother Nature."

Very slowly I opened the door to the loose box and stepped inside, clutching the bag of golden Delicious apples I'd brought. Would Ariel remember me? It had only been three days since I'd seen her, but she'd been through a lot during that short time. Maybe we'd have to get acquainted all over again.

I needn't have worried. Ariel came right over to me, favoring her left hind leg just a little, and whuffled a greeting. I gently put my arms around her, resting my cheek on her satiny neck. "You're still beautiful," I told her, blinking back my tears. "You'll always be my dream horse, no matter what."

I would have been content to stand like that for hours, but Ariel wasn't. She had sniffed out the apples, and she made it very clear that it was time for her treat.

As I fed them to her slice by slice—they were kind of limp because they'd been sitting in my locker all day—my eyes kept being drawn to the long, jagged line of stitches that marred her sleek golden side. If I could have gotten my hands on the person who'd let Ariel and the other horses out, I would cheerfully have strangled him without one bit of guilt!

I guess Zach felt the same way, because when I asked him to meet Lydia and me at Basta Pizza the

146

next day to figure out the next step in our investigation, he agreed right away.

Lydia and I got to the pizza parlor first and snagged a table by the window. The place was pretty full—it was a favorite hangout for the kids from Stockton High, and a lot of Whitfield College students ate there too. As soon as Zach arrived, we ordered our pizza and sodas. Then we got down to business.

"Okay," I said. "We know Joanna Talley's innocent. That leaves the bikers and the Putnams."

"Don't forget Mr. Brewster," Lydia added.

Zach groaned. "Not that again! Get real, Lydia."

"I thought the idea of this meeting was to explore all the possibilities," Lydia said, "and you can't deny that Mr. Brewster *is* a possibility."

"Listen, you guys," I said quickly, before Zach could retort. "Let's not waste time arguing. We'll keep Mr. Brewster on the list, but for the moment I think we'd better concentrate on the others. Now, since the bikers seem to have disappeared, I think our best bet is to zero in on the Putnams and—"

"Speak of the devil!" Lydia interrupted. Then she giggled. "Or at least, the devil's son. Look who just walked in—Edward Brewster!"

Sure enough, there was Edward, and he was coming our way. As usual, every hair was in place. His chinos were immaculate, and he was wearing a beautifully tailored tweed jacket.

147

"Hi, Tess, Lydia," he said, stopping beside our table. Smiling at Zach, he added, "I don't believe I've met your friend."

After I introduced him to Zach and they shook hands, Edward said to me, "I haven't seen you since the disaster at your uncle's stable, but Sabrina and I have talked about it a lot. She told me that the palomino was injured. I'm sorry, Tess. I know you're really crazy about her."

"Thanks, Edward," I said. "Ariel was pretty badly hurt, but she's doing much better now."

"That's great! Sabrina also told me that Mr. Sherrill and Joanna Talley are getting married. I'm looking forward to meeting them both one of these days. Are they going to live at his place or hers?"

"I don't think they've decided yet," I said.

"You know," Edward said thoughtfully, "under the circumstances, it would make a lot of sense if your uncle accepted Dad's offer and moved to Greenbriar. With the money my father's willing to pay for his property, he and Ms. Talley could merge their assets and get her stable on sound financial footing. . . ." He broke off, grinning sheepishly. "I guess you can tell that my last class was business economics, right? What I should have said was, I hope Mr. Sherrill and Ms. Talley will be very happy."

Just then a guy of about Edward's age came over to him and slapped him on the back. "Hey, Brewster, you owe me an explanation! I thought you were coming to the Phi Delt party Saturday night, and you never showed. I called you a couple of times, but nobody answered. What happened? Running around with some other chick while your girlfriend was out of town?"

Edward turned brick red. Glancing at me, he said, "Sabrina's *sister* knows I would never do anything like that!"

"Oh—Sabrina's sister," the other guy muttered. "Sorry about that, Brewster. Well, guess I'll be going. A bunch of us have a booth in the back. Come join us when you're through here—if you're still talking to me, that is."

As he headed for the rear of the pizza parlor, Edward said earnestly, "You *do* know I wouldn't go out with any other girl, don't you, Tess?"

Before I could reply, Lydia exclaimed, "Oh, good! Here comes our pizza. I'm starved!"

"I'd better be going too," Edward said. He still looked uncomfortable. "See you. Nice meeting you, Zach."

"Yeah, you too."

"Now, where were we?" I said.

"We were talking about the Putnams," Lydia reminded me.

"Right. Here's my plan. On Saturday we ride over to their place and try to snoop around. It won't be easy, because there are three of them, but listen to this! Lydia pretends that she's fallen off her horse—"

"I can't," Lydia cut in.

149

"What do you mean, you can't? You don't *really* fall off. You dismount where nobody can see you, and then . . ."

Lydia shook her head. Through a mouthful of pizza she mumbled, "That's not the problem. Jeremy and I are going on a hike with this walking club he belongs to. We're taking a picnic, and we won't be back until late."

"Who's Jeremy?" Zach asked.

"A friend of Lydia's," I said with a sigh. "A friend who's apparently a member of every organization in town."

"Oh, Tess, he is not!" Lydia protested. "He's multifaceted, that's all. Jeremy's broadening my horizons. It's not that I don't want to help you guys, but I've already made these plans. I can't cancel them now."

I couldn't argue with her. After all, Lydia *was* my best friend, no matter what, and I didn't want to spoil things with her first real boyfriend. Turning to Zach, I said, "Then we'll do it by ourselves. If it's okay with you, that is."

Zach reached for a second slice of pizza. "Sure. Tell me more about your plan."

So I did. I had to revise it a little since Lydia wouldn't be going with us, and though Zach wasn't wildly enthusiastic, he agreed that it might work. In spite of Lydia's refusal to take part in it, he insisted on paying for her pizza and mine as well as his own, and our sodas, too. I thought that was awfully nice of him.

We were walking out the door of Basta Pizza when we heard the roar of motorcycle engines on Kent Street.

Lydia's eyes widened. "This time it *is* them! The Panthers! They've come back!"

¬11¬

But the three bikers who barreled into the parking lot didn't look anything like the ones who had given us so much trouble at The Barn. Though they all had on black-leather jackets with silver studs, the jackets didn't say "Panthers" on the back. None of them were big and beefy like Ace, and only one of them, a scrawny guy, was wearing a helmet.

"That's not them," Zach said, starting down the steps. "Come on—I'll give you both a lift home."

Lydia scurried after him while I followed more slowly. As the bikers sauntered toward the pizza parlor, I got a closer look at the boy in the bright-blue helmet. I have a pretty good memory for faces, and I recognized his right away.

"Tess, where are you going?" Lydia cried as I shot past her and Zach.

I didn't answer. Planting myself in front of the skinny biker, I said, "Fallen off any horses lately?"

"Hey, Spider, who's this? Your girlfriend?" sniggered a fat, pimply guy with too much hair.

"I've never seen her before in my life!"

The boy called Spider tried to edge around me, but Zach, Lydia, and I blocked his path. "Oh yes you have," I said. "Remember when the Panthers rented horses a few weeks ago and the mare you were riding ran away with you? I was the one who caught her."

"I *told* you it was them!" Lydia exclaimed. "At least it's one of them."

Spider stared at all of us, his pale-blue eyes bulging. He remembered all right, but he wasn't going to admit it. "I don't know what you're talking about," he blustered. "What are you, nuts?"

A tall, lanky biker with hardly any hair at all grabbed Zach's shoulder, growling, "You got a problem, man?"

"No, but you will if you don't get your paws off me, *man*," Zach said, clenching his fists. Compared to him, the other boy looked pretty puny. "Now why don't you and your pal go order your food while you still have teeth to eat it with? We want to have a little talk with Spider here."

The guy backed off, and after a mumbled consultation with the fat one, they both headed for the pizza parlor.

"Hey, fellas, where you going?" Spider yelped with a nervous glance at Zach. "Come back!"

"Are you sure you want them to come back?" I asked sweetly. "Because if they do, I'll be happy to tell them how scared you were of that nice, gentle horse, and how a *girl* had to rescue you!"

As the door closed behind his friends, Spider's thin shoulders slumped. "Why are you picking on me?" he whined. "What did I ever do to you?"

"That's what we want to find out," Zach said grimly. "How about answering some questions? For starters, where do the Panthers hang out?"

Spider scowled. "How should I know?"

Zach seized the front of his jacket, glaring down at him. "You should know because you're a member of their gang. Now tell us—*where do they hang out?*"

"I don't know. I'm *not* a member of their gang," Spider said sullenly. "I never saw those guys before that day, and I've only seen them once since. I met them on the highway near Danbury—that's where I live—and they let me ride with them for a while, that's all. After you and Ace had that fight, he made a lot of noise about getting back at you and the guy who owns the stable, but some of the others talked him out of it. They said it wasn't worth hanging around the sticks just to beat up a couple of hick farmers. . . ." Zach tightened his grip on Spider's jacket, and Spider cringed. "*I* didn't say it—*they* did! Anyway, they went back to New York, and I went home."

155

Zach let him go. "The Panthers are from New York?"

Spider nodded. "Yeah—Yonkers, I think they said. Are you ever gonna tell me what this is all about?"

"Somebody began causing a lot of trouble at my uncle's stable a week after you and the Panthers were there," I explained. "My friends and I thought maybe the Panthers were trying to get revenge."

"No way," Spider said. "Those guys went to some big motorcycle rally upstate the next Saturday. I saw them there. I'm sure they didn't plan on coming back to Stockton." Glaring at Zach, he asked, "Any more questions?"

Zach shrugged. "Nope. Feel free to get your pizza."

Spider scuttled away very fast. Pausing by the entrance to the pizza parlor, he smoothed the front of his leather jacket, settled his helmet more firmly on his head, and squared his shoulders. Cocky now that he was out of Zach's reach, he turned around. "Those horses are dangerous!" he yelled. "They oughta close that stable down before somebody gets killed!"

"What a nasty little wimp," I muttered as Zach, Lydia, and I headed for Zach's car. "I wish I *hadn't* rescued him!"

"Well, I guess we can scratch the Panthers from our list," Lydia said as she got into the backseat. I sat in front, next to Zach. "If Spider's telling the truth— and even though he's a pretty slimy character, I

156

don't know why he'd lie about it—they have an alibi for the time The Barn was graffitied. And it doesn't seem likely that they did anything else, either."

"Yeah—they'd have to be pretty determined to ride all the way from Yonkers to Stockton and back in one night," Zach agreed. "It looks like the Putnams are the only suspects left."

After a couple of tries he coaxed the engine to life, and the car sputtered and wheezed its way out of the lot onto Kent Street.

"I'm not going to say a single word about Mr. Brewster," Lydia said.

Zach sighed. "You just did."

"I know. But it's the last time I'll mention him. I've been thinking—even if he was behind the whole thing, we'd probably never be able to prove it. I'm sure he'd provide ironclad alibis for whoever he hired, so there's not much point in checking him out. Right, Tess?"

When I didn't reply, she leaned over the seat and waved a hand in front of my face. "Tess? Hello? Wake up!"

"I guess," I murmured. I'd been listening, but I'd been thinking, too. Several things had been bothering me for some time now, and Lydia's talk about alibis suddenly made them all fall into place. There was one person who wasn't on our list, and that person didn't have an alibi for either of the nights in question. But I wasn't ready to mention his name to Lydia and Zach, because I really hoped I was wrong.

* * *

Saturday was the beginning of the long Columbus Day weekend, when The Barn usually did good business. But there were very few riders, so Zach and I took out only one small party that morning. I spent the rest of the time grooming Ariel and helping Matthew and Orville with stable chores.

After lunch I led the palomino to one of the paddocks so she could get some exercise. Bill, the sheriff's deputy, came over to watch. He was supposed to be standing guard, but he didn't seem to take his responsibility very seriously. As Ariel trotted around me in a circle at the end of the long lunge line, she tossed her head, swished her silvery tail, and picked up her hooves as if there was nothing wrong with her at all.

"That sure is a beautiful horse," Bill said admiringly. "Too bad about the scar, but it looks like Doc Ryan fixed her up pretty good. Guess you'll be able to ride her again soon."

"Not for a while yet," I told him. "Ariel can't be ridden until her wound is completely healed." *And she can't be driven to New Jersey in a van until then either*, I thought. As far as I knew, Matthew still hadn't heard from Mr. Graham. But that didn't mean he wouldn't show up one of these days to claim his horse.

Ariel was getting better and better every day. Next Wednesday, if all went well, the vet would probably remove her stitches, and soon there would be nothing to prevent Mr. Graham from taking my dream horse away. I tried to concentrate on The Barn mystery instead of thinking about this awful possibility.

Around mid-afternoon Matthew suggested that Zach and I take a break and go for a ride by ourselves. That was exactly what we'd been waiting to hear. We saddled up Moonshine and Lucky and started out for Eli Putnam's farm.

"Wouldn't it be great if Old Man Putnam and his sons went away for the weekend?" I said as we rode side by side. "A lot of people do. Then we could take a really good look around."

Zach shook his head. "I bet the Putnams don't. If we're lucky, they'll be out in the fields, but we can't count on it. I guess we'll have to stick with your crazy plan."

"It's not crazy," I said, frowning. "You said yourself it could work. Maybe it won't work as well without Lydia, but there's nothing we can do about that."

My original strategy had been for us to tie our horses out of sight. Then Lydia would limp up to the Putnams' farmhouse, saying she'd been thrown. I figured she could pretend to faint, or throw a fit, or something—Lydia would have been good at that. While Mr. Putnam, Charles, and Henry were distracted, Zach and I would sneak over to the barn and outbuildings and snoop around, searching for incriminating evidence. But since there were only two of us, I'd have to play Lydia's part, leaving Zach to do the sneaking and snooping on his own.

We reined our horses to a stop in a grove of trees at the end of a short, rutted track that led to the Putnam farm. It sure was a grungy-looking place. The ramshackle barn and the sheds surrounding it might once have been red, but they hadn't been painted in years, and the farmhouse wasn't in much better shape. The yard in front of the house was overgrown with weeds and littered with old tires, the rusted chassis of an ancient car, and a lot of other junk that I couldn't identify.

"I don't see their truck," I said to Zach. "Looks like they're not home. Let's ride a little closer." I began walking Lucky down the lane, keeping an eye out for any signs of life, but all I saw were some cows grazing in a rocky pasture nearby.

Zach followed me on Moonshine. "Tess, I don't think this is such a hot idea. I thought the plan was for us to hide the horses and then walk."

"Well, it was, but since nobody's around . . ."

Before I could finish my sentence, a voice shouted from behind us, "Get off Putnam property! You're trespassing, and trespassers deserve to be shot!"

Terrified, I whirled Lucky around and saw Charles Putnam walking quickly toward us down the lane. He had a rifle in his hands, and two mangy dogs raced ahead of him, barking and growling and making straight for Zach and me. I could tell that, unlike Nemo and Flash, those dogs didn't just *look* fierce.

They *were* fierce, and I was glad we were on horseback instead of on foot. Even so, we were trapped. We couldn't go back the way we'd come because Charles was in the way, and Mr. Putnam was running around the corner of the barn with Henry and an even bigger, meaner-looking dog at his heels.

"You were right," I muttered to Zach as we tried to calm our nervous horses. "It was a crazy plan!"

Mr. Putnam and Henry were closing in on us now, and I said the first thing that popped into my head. "Afternoon, Mr. Putnam," I called in a quavering voice. "It's Tess Sherrill and Zach Wallace. Would you please ask Charles not to shoot us?" To my relieved surprise, he did.

"Charley, put that dad-blamed gun away!" Mr. Putnam bellowed. "You was supposed to be hunting rabbits, not kids! Henry, call off them dogs!"

Henry glared at us. "Why? They're trespassing, like Charley said."

"Just do it!" his father ordered.

All three dogs were circling Moonshine and Lucky, snarling and baring their sharp teeth. When one of them came too close, Lucky lashed out with a hind hoof, kicking it squarely in the side. The dog let out a yelp of pain and slunk away, whimpering like a hurt puppy. Giving Zach and me a murderous look, Henry ran after it, whistling to the other two.

"You kids better get on home before I set the law on you!" Mr. Putnam said. "What're you doing here, anyway?"

161

I was tongue-tied, but Zach managed to come up with a believable response. "I guess you heard about Matthew Sherrill's horses being let loose last Saturday night," he said. "We just thought we'd stop by and find out if there's been any trouble at your place too."

Old Man Putnam frowned and scratched his beard. "No, there ain't, but I heard about your trouble, and I been mighty worried. I don't want none of my livestock driven off like that. I got cows and pigs and chickens, and that's *all* I got until that Brewster fella buys my land. I told my boys to keep watch and make sure nobody tries anything. Guess that's why Charley acted like he did when he saw you." He looked up at me. "You tell your uncle I'm still mad at him and I'm still gonna sue him as soon as I find me a lawyer, but I never wished his horses any harm."

"I'll tell him, Mr. Putnam," I said. "I'm sorry we disturbed you."

Zach and I turned our horses around and trotted back down the lane. As we passed Charles, I forced a friendly smile, but he didn't return it.

After we had ridden in silence for a while, Zach said glumly, "Well, the *good* news is we're still in one piece. The *bad* news is, we didn't find out anything about the Putnams at all, and it doesn't look like we'll get another chance. I guess from now on we'd better just leave the investigation up to Sheriff Griswold."

162

"Maybe," I said.

Zach glanced suspiciously at me. "What do you mean, maybe? You're not hatching another one of your far-out schemes, are you?"

I gave him my version of Lydia's wide-eyed innocent stare. "Who, me?"

"Yes, you. Listen, Tess," he said earnestly, "I know how much you want to find whoever's responsible for what happened to Ariel and Midnight. I want to find them too. But let's face it—we're fresh out of suspects. There's nothing more we can do."

For a moment I was tempted to tell Zach about the person on my own private list, but I didn't. He'd probably just laugh at me, and as far as I was concerned, this was no laughing matter. So I just said, "I suppose you're right. There's nothing we can do."

But that didn't mean there was nothing *I* could do.

When we rode into the stable yard a few minutes later, I saw tethered to the split-rail fence a big chestnut gelding with a white blaze on his forehead. I was sure I'd never seen that horse before. As Zach and I dismounted, I wondered who the chestnut belonged to. But I didn't have to wonder long, because just then Joanna Talley came out of the office. She was wearing a heavy Irish sweater, tan riding pants, and tall, glossy boots, and her long blond hair was tied back at the nape of her neck. She smiled when she saw me.

"Who's that?" Zach whispered as she came toward us.

163

"*That* is the dragon lady," I whispered back, grinning at the look of astonishment on his face.

"Just the people I wanted to see," Joanna said. "Hi, Tess. And you must be Zach Wallace. I'm Joanna Talley. I've heard so much about you from Matthew."

Zach shook the hand she extended to him, mumbling, "Pleased to meet you."

"Matthew and I would like you to join us for dinner on Monday," Joanna continued. Turning to me, she added, "Your parents, your sister, and Sabrina's boyfriend are coming too, Tess. I guess you might call it an engagement party. Matthew decided it was time we all tried to forget about our problems for at least one evening. I'm really looking forward to it."

"Sounds great," I said, and Zach nodded.

Joanna smiled at us both. "Terrific! About six o'clock, okay?" She went over to the chestnut, untied him, and swung gracefully into the saddle. "See you then."

Zach gazed after her as she rode away. I guess he was still a little dazed. "So that's Joanna Talley!" he said. "She sure isn't anything like I expected."

As we led our horses into the stable, I suddenly realized that Matthew and Joanna's party might be the perfect opportunity to zero in on my secret suspect. The best engagement present I could give them would be to solve the mystery once and for all.

~12~

My parents and I were the first to arrive on Monday evening. As we drove past the stable on our way to the house, I leaned out the window and waved at Bill the deputy, who was sitting in his car, as usual. It felt strange to be at The Barn without stopping by to see Ariel, and to be wearing a dress instead of my riding clothes—but Mom had insisted that for such a special occasion, we all had to look our best.

She and Sabrina were thrilled about Matthew's upcoming marriage, and Dad was pleased too. They were sure that with the added responsibility of a wife and maybe even children one day, Matthew would settle down at last. My mother had even brought a beautifully wrapped engagement present for him and Joanna, a cut-crystal bowl from Sherrill's Home Decorating department. I couldn't help wondering what they'd do with it. Though I knew they'd appreciate the gift, I didn't think either my uncle or Joanna was the cut-crystal type.

Dad parked the car in front of Matthew's house, and he and my mother started up the walk, with me lagging behind. I was having second thoughts about the decision I'd made on Saturday. It had seemed like such a terrific idea at the time, but now I wasn't so sure. I didn't have any real proof, just a lot of circumstantial evidence and a very strong hunch. But if I could get my secret suspect alone and catch him off guard, maybe he'd blurt out a confession. On the other hand, what if he denied everything? What would I do then?

As Dad knocked on the farmhouse door, Edward's little green sports car pulled up behind my parents' sedan. He and Sabrina got out and hurried up the walk hand in hand just as Joanna opened the door, looking lovely in snug-fitting velvet pants and a white silk shirt.

"Hello," she said, smiling at us all. "Come on in—oh, no!" She grabbed the dogs' collars just in time to prevent Nemo and Flash from jumping all over us, and stepped aside to let us pass, calling over her shoulder, "Matt, our guests are here and I could use a little help with the welcoming committee!"

Matthew came into the hall from the kitchen. He'd had a haircut, and his beard was neatly trimmed. Unlike my father and Edward, he wasn't wearing a

166

suit, but in his tan slacks and Fair Isle sweater, I thought he looked great.

"Nemo, Flash, behave yourselves," he said sternly. Then he turned to us, smiling broadly. "Now it's *my* turn to welcome you, but I promise I won't knock you down."

After kisses, handshakes, and introductions all around, Matthew put our coats in the hall closet. "Somebody's missing," he said. "Where's Zach?"

"He said he was coming," I told him, "but I wouldn't be surprised if that so-called car of his had a problem. Maybe I ought to call his house."

I was about to pick up the phone on the table by the stairs when I heard a familiar cough, wheeze, and sputter from outside, followed by a loud *bang*. Everyone jumped, including the dogs, and Sabrina let out a little shriek.

"Was that—was that a gunshot?" my mother asked.

Laughing, I said, "No, that was Zach's car. It backfires a lot." Flash, Nemo, and I ran to the door, but when I opened it, I saw a stranger standing there—a tall, handsome, well-dressed stranger.

"Hi, Tess," he said. "Sorry I'm late. Had a little trouble getting the heap started. *Down*, fellas," he told the dogs. "This is my best jacket, and I'd like to wear it again sometime."

I blinked. "Zach?"

"Yeah. Who did you think it was?" He grinned at me. "Can I come in? It's kind of chilly out here."

167

"Yes—sure—come on in." Still a little dazed, I introduced him to my parents and my sister.

We all followed Joanna into the living room then, and Sabrina murmured in my ear, "Aren't you the sneaky one! Now I know the *real* reason you spend so much time at The Barn. Zach's really cute!"

I could feel my face turning beet red. "That's not the reason at all," I whispered. But I had to admit she was right about Zach, and when he sat next to me on the sofa in front of the fireplace, my heart gave a funny little flutter. *It's just nerves*, I told myself. *I'm nervous about carrying out my plan. It has absolutely nothing to do with Zachary Wallace.*

But as I nibbled at the hors d'oeuvres Matthew had prepared and sipped Joanna's herb tea, I began to relax, letting the conversation swirl around me. Everybody was having a good time, and they all had a lot to say, so nobody seemed to notice that I wasn't saying anything at all.

At last my mother presented Joanna with the gift she'd brought. Joanna lifted the bowl out of its tissue-paper nest, an expression of wonder on her face. "I can't believe it," she said softly. "Mama had one just like this, and when I was a little girl, I broke it. I swore I'd replace it one day, but I never did. Thank you for doing it for me, Sylvia."

"Thank you both," Matthew said, smiling at my parents. He placed the bowl in the center of the mantel. "And now I think it's about time for supper."

"You okay, Tess?" Zach asked as Joanna led the

way to the dining room. "You haven't said a word all evening, and that's not like you."

"I'm fine," I said. "I was just listening and—thinking about things."

He frowned. "What things? You're not up to something, are you? And don't give me that 'Who, me?' routine. I've seen that look on your face before, and it usually means trouble."

"I haven't the faintest idea what you're talking about," I said airily, taking a seat at the table. But I was pretty sure he didn't believe me.

Though the meal was delicious, I couldn't eat much of it. My stomach had tied itself into a knot. If I was going to confront my suspect, I'd have to do it soon, and I wasn't looking forward to it. Picking at my food, I was lost in thought until the mention of my name brought me back to the present.

". . . and as I was telling Tess the other day, Mr. Sherrill, if you sell your place to Dad, you and Ms. Talley could invest the proceeds in Greenbriar," Edward was saying. "My father agrees that it would be a shrewd move on your part." He leaned forward eagerly. "Dad's really got his heart set on building Brewster Estates. Supermarkets and shopping malls won't put the family name on any map, but Brewster Estates will. Can't I persuade you to reconsider? If there's any way I can make Dad's dream come true, I want to give it a shot."

Matthew nodded. "I understand, Edward, and your devotion to your father does you credit. But if

169

you don't mind, I'd rather not discuss it at the moment. This is supposed to be a celebration, not a business conference." His smile took some of the sting out of his words, but not all. Edward's face flushed and he sat back in his chair, looking like a child who had been scolded.

"Well!" Joanna said brightly, breaking the uncomfortable silence. "While I clear the table and make the coffee, why don't the rest of you adjourn to the living room? We can have dessert in front of the fire."

"Good idea," Matthew said as everyone stood up. "Need a hand, Jo?"

"No, she doesn't," I said quickly. "I mean, Joanna shouldn't be stuck in the kitchen at her own engagement party. I'll do all that stuff, and Edward will help me, won't you, Edward?"

"Yes, of course. Be glad to," Edward said, giving me a grateful glance.

Zach and Sabrina offered to help too, but I shooed them out of the dining room.

Edward and I began stacking plates and cutlery. "Thanks, Tess," he mumbled. "Maybe by the time dessert's ready, your uncle will have forgiven me for acting like such a jerk. I didn't mean to ruin the party."

I didn't reply until the kitchen door had closed behind us and we had put the dirty dishes in the sink. Then I turned to face him. "You didn't ruin the party," I said. "But you've been trying very hard to ruin Matthew, haven't you?"

"What?" Edward stared at me in astonishment. "What do you mean?"

I moved a step closer to him. "Just now you said you'd do anything to make your father's dream come true, and the only way you can do that is by forcing my uncle out of business!"

"Now wait a minute, Tess. You don't think . . ."

"I *do* think," I said. "I've been thinking a lot lately, and remembering things too. To begin with, where were you the night the stable was graffitied?" He just gaped at me. "It was a Friday night early last month."

"I—I don't know," he stammered. "I guess I was out with Sabrina. We always go out on Friday nights."

"Not that Friday night you didn't! I remember, because she was all upset about you breaking your date." Before he could speak, I said, "Then there's the night of the Harvest Moon Trail Ride. You told me that afternoon when you came to The Barn that you had to cram for a big test, so you wouldn't be going anywhere. But your friend at the pizza parlor said he'd tried to call you several times and nobody answered. Where were you then? Where were you when somebody shot off a gun in the woods, and later, when the horses were let out and Ariel and Midnight were hurt? *Where were you, Edward?*"

My voice had risen, and Edward grabbed me by

171

the arms. "Will you pipe down?" he hissed. "Next thing you know, we'll have everybody in here! Believe me, Tess, you're wrong."

"Let me go!" I shouted.

Edward released me just as the door swung open and Zach burst in. "What's going on here?" he yelled.

I stumbled into Zach's arms. "It was Edward!" I cried.

Suddenly the kitchen was full of people, all asking questions at once. "Edward? What's Edward done?" "Tess, what's wrong?" "What's all the noise about?" "Is somebody hurt?"

And then in the midst of all the confusion, I heard Matthew saying, "Jo? What is it?"

Joanna was staring intently out the window. Whirling around, she said one terrifying word: *"Fire!"*

She shot out the back door with Matthew and the dogs at her side and my father and Edward close behind. Zach and I followed them, and the minute we got outside, I saw a flickering red-orange glow in the window of the upper level of the barn, where all the hay and straw was stored.

"Oh, no!" I cried. "We've got to put it out! If it spreads, Ariel and the other horses will burn!"

"Get Bill," Zach hollered to my mother and Sabrina, who were bringing up the rear in their high heels. "He's the sheriff's deputy in the car around front. Tell him there's a fire in the stable!" He sprinted ahead. I tried to keep up with him, but his legs were so much longer than mine that it was impossible.

When I raced into the barn moments later, my father and Matthew were using fire extinguishers to quench the last of the hungry flames licking at a stack of hay bales near the window, while Joanna sprayed the walls and floor around them with a hose. The rest of the place was in total darkness, but I heard grunts, thuds, and frantic barking coming from somewhere not far away.

"Where's Zach?" I asked anxiously.

"Helping Edward," Joanna said. "Edward tackled somebody, and he's putting up one heck of a fight!" She thrust the hose into my hands, then hit the light switch and ran in the direction of the grunts and thuds.

The bulbs high overhead weren't very bright, and now that the fire was almost out, steam and smoke billowed from the sodden hay and wood, stinging my eyes. At first all I could make out were three shadowy figures grappling in a corner. Then a stiff breeze from the barn's open doorway began to blow the haze away, and I was able to see more clearly.

Zach, Edward, and a wiry guy in a black-leather jacket were rolling around on the straw-covered floor in a tangle of arms and legs while Flash and Nemo danced around them, barking and growling.

Spider! I thought, astonished. It was Spider all along!

Suddenly the one in the jacket flung a handful of dusty straw in Zach's face, at the same time landing a vicious kick on Edward's shin. He scrambled to his feet. Joanna tried to grab him, but he was too quick for her. With another kick at Nemo, he made a headlong dash for the door.

That's when I saw who it actually was. I aimed the jet of water from my hose directly at his thin, weasely face. Coughing and sputtering, the guy staggered backward, tripped over Flash, and fell. I heard a solid *clunk* as his head hit the floor. Joanna promptly sat on his chest, Edward grabbed his arms, and Zach pinned down his legs just as Bill, my mother, and Sabrina came running in.

"Hey, Henry," I said. "Was it really worth all this just for a trip to California and a new motorcycle?"

In less than an hour Bill had taken statements from all of us, and from a sullen, defiant Henry Putnam. Henry confessed to everything. Besides setting the fire, he'd spray-painted the barn, fired the shots, and let out the horses all by himself. Neither his older brother nor his father had known anything about it.

"And I'd do it again if I got the chance," Henry yelled as Bill led him in handcuffs to the car. "If we're not gonna be rich, I'd rather go to jail! I don't ever want to go back to that crummy farm!"

After the deputy drove him away, Dad, Matthew, and Zach made sure the fire was completely out while Joanna started back to the house with my mother, Sabrina, and Edward. Hurrying after Edward, I tapped him hesitantly on the shoulder. He turned around, giving me a quizzical look. With his suit all rumpled and his hair standing on end, he certainly didn't look like one of the store's mannequins anymore!

"Uh—Edward, about all those things I said after dinner . . ." I mumbled. "I'm really sorry. I wouldn't blame you if you never spoke to me again."

"Yes—what was all the yelling about, anyway?" Sabrina asked, frowning.

I swallowed hard. "Well, you see, I thought Edward—"

"Your sister was mad at me because she thought I'd fouled up your uncle's engagement party," Edward cut in quickly. "And she was right. I should have kept my big mouth shut about Brewster Estates." He smiled and held out a hand to me. "No hard feelings, Tess?"

I shook his hand gratefully. "No hard feelings. Thanks, Edward!"

As Edward and Sabrina walked up to the house, I ran back to the barn. Matthew and Zach had already gone down to the lower level to calm the horses, knowing that all the noise and smoke must have spooked them.

I went straight to the palomino's stall and flung my arms around her neck. "It's over, Ariel," I whispered as I gently stroked the jittery mare. "There's nothing to be afraid of anymore. As long as you're here, everything's going to be all right."

As long as you're here. But I knew that at any moment Mr. Graham might come back, and no matter how much I loved her, I'd have to give her up.

I was feeling pretty depressed when Zach stuck his head into the palomino's stall a few minutes later. Even though his best jacket was a mess, his shirt was ripped, and his tie was askew, he was grinning from ear to ear. "Ready for dessert, Tess?" he asked. "Now we *really* have something to celebrate!"

I didn't want my worries about losing Ariel to put a damper on everyone else's high spirits. Forcing a smile, I reached up and picked a few pieces of straw out of Zach's touseled hair. "Come on, Scarecrow," I said. "Let's go!"

~13~

On the Saturday night before Halloween, we all gathered at the barn again. But this time the upper level was decorated with fat orange pumpkins and corn shocks, and orange-and-black crepe-paper streamers were festooned from the rafters. All my friends were there in costume. Witches and cowboys, gypsies and ghosts, princesses and mummies danced to the music pouring from the speakers of Matthew's CD player. More oddly-assorted couples crowded around the refreshment table, where Orville was helping Dad serve the cookies Joanna and my mother had baked and the punch Sabrina had made. Everybody had joined forces to give me a birthday party I'd never forget.

A tall black cat in glasses came over to me, leading *Star Trek*'s Mr. Spock by the hand. He was wearing glasses too. "Tess, you look *gorgeous*," the cat exclaimed. "I just knew you'd be a perfect Scarlett O'Hara. Isn't she perfect, Jeremy? Tess's sister and I made her costume."

Mr. Spock smiled and nodded, and one of his pointed ears almost fell off. "A lovely flower of the Confederacy," he said gallantly. "Why don't I get you ladies some punch?"

As Jeremy moved away, adjusting his ear, Lydia gave me a big hug. "Happy birthday, Tess! How does it feel to be fifteen?"

I laughed. "I'm not sure yet. I haven't been fifteen for very long." Standing on tiptoe, I scanned the crowd. "You haven't seen Zach anywhere, have you?"

"No, but I'm sure he's on his way. He's probably having car trouble again," Lydia said. "You know he wouldn't miss your birthday party for the world." Then she whispered, "And you know something else? He's nuts about you, and I think you're nuts about him, too!"

I felt my face turning bright red. "He's not! I'm not!" I protested weakly.

Lydia just grinned at me, and in spite of myself I found myself grinning back. "Well, I guess maybe I'm a *little* nuts about him," I confessed. Then my smile faded. "But as far as I can tell, Zach doesn't even know I'm a girl!"

"Oh, Tess, he does so—even though you haven't given him a whole lot of help until tonight. When he sees you in that dress, it's really going to blow his mind."

I sighed. "*If* he sees me in this dress."

"Believe me, he will," Lydia assured me. "I have a hunch he'll be here very soon."

"I sure hope so," I said. "After all, it's not only my birthday, but also kind of a farewell to The Barn, even though Matthew won't be moving the horses to Greenbriar until after he and Joanna are married."

My uncle's decision to sell his land had taken some getting used to. But he explained that after several long consultations over the past couple of weeks, Mr. Brewster had promised to make a thorough environmental-impact survey of Matthew's and Mr. Putnam's properties before breaking ground for Brewster Estates. At Edward's urging, his father had also agreed to build fewer houses than he'd originally planned and to make them as energy efficient as possible. Mr. Brewster had even hired Matthew as a consultant on harnessing solar power for heat and hot water.

"So I guess the Putnams will be going to California after all," Lydia said. "Except Henry, that is."

"Oh, Henry's going too," I told her. "But not until he completes a hundred hours of community service. Matthew thinks he'll straighten out. He says Henry's only a kid, and he deserves the chance to make a fresh start." Scowling, I added, "If it was up to me, I'd lock up that little weasel and throw away the key.

I'll never forgive him for what happened to Midnight and Ariel, not if I live to be a thousand!"

"I'm with you," Lydia said. "But let's try to forget about Horrible Henry tonight and concentrate on fun and romance, okay?" She frowned. "Speaking of romance, I wonder where Jeremy is with our punch. I'd better find him before he gets trapped in a time warp with some sexy alien." Picking up her long black tail, she waved it at me and began edging her way around the brightly costumed guests.

Just then somebody tapped me on the shoulder, and a deep voice said in a fake southern accent, "May Ah have this dance, Miz Scawlett?"

I spun around eagerly, hoping it was Zach, but it wasn't. In spite of the clown suit and makeup, I recognized Chuck Fletcher, a guy in my homeroom at school.

"Sure, Chuck," I said, smiling to hide my disappointment.

He looked crestfallen. "How'd you know it was me?"

"I think it was this," I told him solemnly, tweaking the red bulb in the middle of his white face. "I never forget a nose!"

While we danced, I kept on looking for Zach. He'd flatly refused to come in costume, so if he'd been there, I would have seen him right away. The only other people in regular clothes were my parents, Matthew, Joanna, and Orville.

And then I caught a glimpse of a short, stocky,

fair-haired man in a brown suit talking to Matthew near the big double doors. All I could see was his back, but there was something about him that was awfully familiar.

"Mr. Graham!" I gasped. "He's come back!"

Leaving my puzzled partner in the middle of the floor, I hiked up my long, ruffled skirts and dodged around the dancers, heading for the two men. But people kept stopping me, wishing me happy birthday and telling me what a great party it was, and by the time I reached the doors, Matthew and the man in the brown suit were nowhere to be seen. Had they gone down to the stable to load Ariel into a van? I wouldn't let them! Somehow I had to stop Mr. Graham from taking the palomino away!

I was racing toward the stairs when a hand reached out and grabbed the bow of my sash. The hand belonged to Li'l Abner, who said, "Slow down, Tess. There's somebody I want you to meet."

"Not now, Edward, *please*," I begged.

"This will only take a minute," Edward promised. "Dad, this is the birthday girl—Sabrina's sister, Tess."

"The pleasure is all mine, Miss O'Hara," said the man in the brown suit standing beside Daisy Mae. "I've heard a great deal about you from your sister and my son."

I just stared at him, openmouthed.

"Tess, where are your manners?" Daisy Mae hissed. "*Say* something!"

"How do you do, Mr. Brewster," I cried, vigorously shaking the hand he held out to me. "It's *so* nice to meet you! I can't tell you how glad I am that you're not somebody else!"

"You'll have to forgive Tess," Sabrina said with a sigh. "I think all the excitement has addled her brain."

Limp with relief that the man I'd seen wasn't Mr. Graham after all, I sank down on the nearest bale of hay. I hadn't lost Ariel, not yet! And as Scarlett O'Hara said in *Gone With the Wind*, "Tomorrow is another day." Tomorrow I'd ask Zach to help me figure out some way to keep her—but meanwhile, where was he? If Lydia was right and he really cared about me, why wasn't he here?

A loud clanging interrupted my thoughts. The music abruptly stopped, and all the laughter and chatter died away. Joanna put down the cookie sheet she'd been striking with a spoon as Matthew walked to the center of the floor and began to speak.

"Ladies and gentlemen," he said, "as you all know, this party is in honor of Tess Sherrill's fifteenth birthday. But it's also in honor of her courage and her unceasing efforts to discover who was responsible for the acts of sabotage here at The Barn. I'm very proud of my niece, and grateful to her too. And now, if I can find her, I'd like to give her a birthday present." He looked around. "Tess, where are you? Come on over here!"

Blushing, I stood up and made my way through

182

the applauding, smiling throng to my uncle's side. He put an arm around me and kissed the top of my head. Then he grinned down at me. "Well, aren't you going to ask where it is?"

"Uh—okay. Where is it?" I asked shyly. Matthew wasn't holding a box or anything. Maybe it was something very small, like a locket, or a ring. Whatever it was, I knew I'd love it.

"It's coming special delivery," Matthew said, "and if my calculations are correct, it ought to be arriving . . . just . . . about—*now*."

One of the big double doors swung open, and to my amazement a scarecrow stepped inside. Straw stuck out of the holes in his ragged clothes and hung down from his battered hat, framing his handsome, smiling face.

"Zach!" I cried happily. "You *did* come!"

And then I caught my breath, because right behind him, at the end of a bright-red lead line, was a dainty little gold-and-silver horse.

I tore my eyes away from her to stare at Matthew in dazzled disbelief. "You don't mean—you can't mean . . ."

"Ariel's yours, Tess," he said simply. "Happy birthday."

"The lead line's a present from me," Zach added, handing it to me.

Stunned, I touched the palomino's warm, silky neck. "I don't believe it. I just don't believe it," I whispered. Then I turned to Matthew again. "But—but what about Mr. Graham?"

My uncle grinned. "You're not the only detective in the family, Tess. I kept making inquiries until I finally located him. I learned that he never paid for Ariel's board because he simply doesn't have the money—he lost his job in Danbury, and his new job doesn't pay enough to support both his family and a horse. We did some long-distance dickering, and the upshot of it was that Mr. Graham agreed to sell the mare to me for a very reasonable price." He patted the breast pocket of his plaid flannel shirt. "I have the bill of sale right here. So don't worry, Tess. The palomino's yours, free and clear."

I was so choked with joyful tears that all I could do was throw my arms around him and hug him tight—until Ariel nudged me with her nose, letting me know that she was feeling neglected. Then I wiped my eyes and paraded her around so my family and all my friends could see how wonderful she was. My dream horse was really mine at last!

After we had circled the room, somebody turned on the music again, and couples began to dance. I reluctantly allowed Matthew to lead the palomino away, but not very far. He tied her to a stout beam near the refreshment table, where she could watch the festivities.

"Why not?" he said. "It's her party too."

I was feeding Ariel a cookie when I felt a warm hand on my shoulder. This time when I turned around, it *was* Zach, and my heart started pounding like crazy.

"Hi, Scarecrow," I said breathlessly. "I'm glad you could make it."

"I'll have you know I've been here for hours," he informed me with wounded dignity. "Who do you think polished that horse of yours? Me, that's who."

I smiled. "Thanks, Zach. And thanks for the lead line, too."

"There's something else. . . ." He had been hiding one hand behind his back, and now he held out one perfect yellow rose almost the color of Ariel's golden coat. "Happy birthday." Beneath that ridiculous hat, Zach's hazel eyes glowed with a light that made my knees turn to jelly. As I tucked the rose into my sash, he said very softly, "You look beautiful, Tess. Would you like to dance?"

"Oh, yes," I whispered. "I'd like that very much."

The scarecrow took me in his arms, and as we swayed to the beat of the music, I decided that there was definitely something to this romance business after all.